NEEDLE ASH
A TALE OF THE ETERNAL DREAM

BOOK II:
TWILIGHT'S MEMORY

BY
DAVID VAN DYKE STEWART
WITH
ILLUSTRATIONS BY BRAD LYNN

This is a work of fiction. All characters and events portrayed herein are fictitious; any resemblance to actual people, living or dead, is purely coincidental.

Cover design by David Van Dyke Stewart
Illustrations by Brad Lynn
Map by David V. Stewart
Interior design by David V. Stewart
Author Photo by Leah Valentine

CONTENTS

Author's Notes

Needle Ash is a new story that I've written in a universe that is not new. I published another book called *The Water of Awakening* that is set in the same world, but in a different geographic location with a different protagonist (However, there are several characters that make appearances in both stories, though you won't meet them in this volume). While *Needle Ash* is technically a sequel to *Water of Awakening,* reading that previous book is not at all required to understand this story, though you may find value in it, for it provides a great amount of exploration into the nature of the world and the magic within it. It is written in a very different style from this book, utilizing something approximating the idealist style of classic fantasy, rather than the contemporary realist style found in Needle Ash, and may not be to every person's tastes.

Within this volume (and the subsequent ones) you will find art plates by Brad Lynn. One of the things I will point out is the accuracy of the arms and armor he depicts, which is one of the reasons I wanted to work with him (I actually found him through a HEMA group, a mutual interest of ours). You can find more of his work at https://www.facebook.com/BradLynnDrawings/

THE CENTRAL
DIVINE STRAND
IN THE FOURTH DOMINION

NEEDLE ASH

BOOK II:
TWILIGHT'S MEMORY

I: In Search of Twilight's Memory

You are what you have always been
Things are as you have made them

To the wise man, changing the world is easy
It is like weaving grass into a basket;
But to the wise man changing himself is a feat
It is like shaping iron into a sword without a forge

But if man is like a sword, the world is the forge
Death, the quench that finalizes the form, flawed or perfect
But who is the hammer?
You will know, when you meet me on the other side,

That you have always been your own hammer.

-The Apocrypha of Verbus, third proclamation.

Michael rode Calot close behind Sharona, who was working a slow path through the thick brush on Rabble-Rouser, her eyes forward, but focused on nothing in particular. To the left of them, Guissali ambled on his own destrier, the black banner on his lance standing proudly in the strong wind. Palsay and Lange-lo were a little ways ahead, both feeling antsy on the new horses Michael had procured for them. Far off to either side, some fifty yards away, were escorts made of dragoons bearing crossbows along with properly armored cavalry. At the request of Johan, Michael had allowed an elite guard to assist him in case the assassins might return. Angelico, who commanded one of the two mixed-unit echelons, was more of a comfort to him than the presence of the rest, who had failed to protect General Butler and King Eduardo, and even fired upon Michael in error, a moment of shock that returned to Michael frequently when he sat pondering the events of his father's murder.

"What are we looking for, exactly?" Guissali said.

"Remnants," Sharona said.

"Of what?" Guissali said. "Ought I to be looking for horse dung, or what?"

"Remnants of what our progenitors dreamt when they were here," Sharona said. "There will be some piece of it left behind in the mundane world."

"That didn't quite answer my question," Guissali said.

"What do you mean by them *dreaming*?" Michael asked. "You say these things often, but always there is some veiled meaning."

"The world is as the dreamers have made it," Sharona said, her eyes wandering over the brush. "We are dreamers, too, or were, once. The dark elves, which were our forebears, created for themselves the world that is, Midgard and its sister realms, but it has become very different from how it was, for the dreamers that followed remade it according to their own wishes." She looked up to the racing clouds for a moment. "Our world has become mundane with the repetition of short human lives, you see: set and difficult to change. The Prim is dry, save for in the Fay Lands. There is little flowing from them to make things of novelty, or to change much of the world.

"And so many of the dark elves have made for themselves schisms in the world that is, remnants of how the world once was. There must be one nearby, a piece of their realm that they returned to when they fled."

"Quite an interesting myth," Guissali said. "But what exactly should I be looking for?"

"You ought to feel more than look," Sharona said. "But if you must look, look for things that don't belong here. There may be ruins, foundations of buildings long gone. Their land is clearly wooded, unlike this plain. An out of place tree, or rock. Use your imagination."

They crested a hill and looked down into a small valley of dry grass and sandstone.

"Just looks the same," Guissali said. "I believe there is a village over yonder though, beyond those hills. Perhaps we could get something to eat there."

"Good idea," Sharona said. "We could ask the people there."

"Would they tell us?" Michael said. "If they have returned from the city of Forgoroto, that is."

"Maybe they'll tell us ghost stories," Sharona said.

Guissali snorted. "If you need ghost stories, you can find plenty among the green and the grey with the Army."

"Besides being entertaining, those kind of stories are often a memory unto themselves." Sharona chuckled softly.

"Ghosts, eh?" Langelo said. His horse moved beneath him as he waited for Michael to approach.

"They looked like ghosts," Michael said. "These elf assassins. They were blurry, like looking at a reflection in a rippling pond, for lack of a better analogy." Michael stopped and shielded his eyes from the sun. "What's that there?" He waived to the cluster of horsemen led by Angelico, and they paused.

"What do you see?" Sharona said, her eyes searching the ground.

Michael rode up beside her and leaned toward her in the saddle. "That, over there." He pointed downhill toward a large cluster of green thistle, but just visible within it was what looked like square stone.

"Yes, good eyes," Sharona said.

They rode down together, followed by the others, to the thistle grove. Sharona dismounted and got close to the dry plants, trying to see the stone below them.

"Guissali," she said. "Please assist me by moving these thorny bushes aside."

"What?"

"You're wearing armor," Sharona said. "If it stops swords, it ought to stop a few thorns."

"Assist the lady," Michael said. "Or are you not a nobleman?"

Guissali groaned and dismounted, his armor clinking. With a grumble, he grabbed the bushes and uprooted two of them, struggling against the hard-packed earth and the long hairy roots that refused to give up their purchase.

"These thorns are still bitey, madam," he huffed. "Why didn't you just burn them all up? I thought you were a mage."

"Because that might burn what is below," Sharona said. She approached and put a hand on Guissali, who paused what he was doing. "It is cut stone. The remnants of a pillar. I don't feel any magic here, though. Can we look around for more?"

After a few minutes hard search, they located another pillar foundation, but nothing more.

"Not enough to lead us into the schism of the realm," Sharona said with a sigh. "That was a proper sight, though. I'm sure we're getting close, so don't feel too bad about it."

"I didn't feel anything except prickly thorns," Guissali said as he struggled back onto his horse.

"Perhaps you need armor of a higher quality or better fit," Sharona said. "Men tend to grow sideways. Is there such a thing as an armor tailor?"

Guissali huffed and grumbled under his breath, "Fickle women."

Palsay cleared this throat. "I don't know of anyone building something around here that would require pillars like that. There's never been a city here."

"Clearly not never," Sharona said. "Like I said, the world has changed much since our forebears created it and dwelt within it. There are many histories the church does not recognize."

"Sure," Palsay said, smirking to Langelo.

"Mind your manners with the lady," Guissali said.

*

The village was either further away than Guissali had figured, or else they were going painfully slow, for they only reached it once the sun was far into the west, stretching their shadows long out to their sides. The dark shapes rippled on the waving grass like it was water, and the younger men watched constantly, as if hypnotized by the motion. Guissali had grown hungry enough to eat a small meal of dried fruit in the saddle. He was far from refusing a second meal when they found evidence of people, and rushed ahead at the first sign of a settlement.

It was a large cluster of houses in a mixture of styles. Some were stone, set in the rolling hills with turf roofs. Others were tall two-story buildings of wood and plaster and shake roofs. Many of the homes were empty, as not all the residents who had fled to the city in advance of the Artalland army had yet returned. All around the town were fields of crops and groves of fruit trees, growing steadily toward harvest unmolested. Amid the irrigated fields and surrounding the houses were nut trees, shading most of the commons.

Being a small village, there was no inn, but there was a large homely house that agreed to feed and house the officers in exchange for pay, though there were not enough cooks (or food) to serve both sets of Angelico's retinue, who made a hasty camp on a nearby hill. The dragoons plied their own suppers from other families or set about to making a meal for themselves from their own stores.

Angelico, Sharona, and Guissali sat with Michael in the large living room of the homely house, watching the fire crackle in a large hearth set into the wall. A kettle had been set over the fire to boil for tea, though it seemed to take its time getting hot. The goodwife, a portly woman named Mura with graying hair, entered with a stack of simple earthenware cups. She placed them on an occasional table and picked up the kettle with a quilted towel just as it started to whistle.

As she strained the tea into the cups she said casually, "What brings such finely arrayed men to Havara?"

"And women," Sharona said.

Mura smiled. "Of course. My apologies."

Angelico caught Michael's eye, as if questioning whether they should tell the woman, but Guissali missed the gesture and spoke straight away. "We're in pursuit of assassins."

"There be none here," the goodwife said, and handed Guissali a cup of tea.

"I did not mean to infer so, my good woman," Guissali replied. "I was merely stating our eventual aim. This stop is…" He turned to look at Michael's face, saw in it a careful frown and said, "Just a stop, madam."

"Do you have any children?" Sharona asked, accepting her teacup.

"Seven. Why?" said Mura.

"I was just curious, since you have such a large house."

"Well, the oldest four have their own houses now. An empty house gets a little quiet, but my youngest are still here, and boisterous as their brothers and sisters."

"I don't hear them," Michael said.

"Oh, they're out with their father at the moment, doing some necessary things that we had to neglect when we feared a real siege."

"I'm glad, then, that a siege did not come to pass," Angelico said. "Though I think our assassins wish enmity between our peoples."

"Enmity is the prerogative of nobility," Mura said. "We in Havara just want to be left to our peace, no matter from whom."

Angelico nodded and sipped his tea.

"Would it be permissible to give your children gifts?" Michael said. "In our country, it is considered proper etiquette to give the children of a homely place a small gift as means of returning the hospitality, but I don't know your own customs."

"Oh, you're welcome to," Mura said with a laugh. "But it's not our custom."

Angelico spoke up, "Then perhaps it would do well to engender some sense of understanding, given that we are now at peace."

"At peace, and soon to have unity of houses," Guissali said, grinning at Michael.

"Oh, I heard rumor of that. It is true, then?" Mura said, taking an empty seat by the fire. "Do you know the prince? Is he as handsome as they say?"

"Know him!" Guissali said. "Why, my lady, you are-" Guissali cut off as he was kicked by Angelico. He cleared his throat. "I am afraid you might be missing the point," he continued. "He is... a most virtuous man. Honest. Fierce... Brave! Kind to the weak. Uh..." Guissali saw Michael's look and quickly sipped his tea. "His character is good, my lady."

"Good. The queen is a fine woman - very kind when she passes through."

"You've seen her, then?" Michael said.

Mura nodded. "She comes and goes often to the country. She was here just a few days ago, too, getting the last bit of outdoor time before the siege, which thankfully didn't end up happening."

"I see," Michael said. "I'm glad she has rapport with the common man."

They sat and discussed idle things for some minutes until the door opened and some children entered along with a tall, lanky man with a black beard. He startled as he entered, especially at Guissali (who had not removed most of his armor), but set about to the kitchen once everyone was introduced. The children were indeed boisterous, ranging in age from eleven (their youngest daughter) to sixteen (a son).

Michael excused himself after the greetings and went outside. He retrieved from his saddlebag a few silver coins. While he was closing the bag back up, Sharona approached.

"What do you think?" he asked, pocketing the coins and standing up.

"I think they're honest. I *do* find it odd that a queen was here."

"Perhaps a little, but I don't know her well... yet. I suppose I will know her," he said with a forced laugh.

Sharona turned and looked to the west, and the growing dusk. "So you *do* intend to marry her."

"It has already been decided."

Sharona turned and began walking back toward the house. "We might as well give those gifts," she said over her shoulder.

Michael frowned, but followed. Inside the house, the children were sitting at the big kitchen table enjoying a supper of hare, apparently caught while they were out patrolling the fields and the sparse wood that ran north of the town.

"Here, I have something for you three, for the furtherment of your house," Michael said, sitting down with the children. He handed each of them two silver coins.

"Two argents each?" said Everani, the youngest and the only girl. "You don't need all this money?"

"It's a nominal sum for a man like me. Keep it safe and spend it wisely," Michael said.

"You must be very rich," the girl said.

"I am in a way, but my life is a little plain. Nothing interesting happens to me, it seems. What about you, is life here interesting?"

"No," said the middle boy, whose name was Jusio. "It's just farming and hunting."

"I heard the queen visited recently," Sharona said. "Is that true?"

"Yeah," the oldest, a tall lad name Butri said. "She's a real pretty one, too. But she didn't stay long."

"Nobody does," Jusio said. "Nothing ever changes around here. Just the same old stuff, day in and day out. That's farming for you."

"That's not true," the girl said. "There are birds. They migrate, and then there's the wandering water."

"Well, I'm going to move to the city," Jusio said. "Where there's always something new to do."

"The city is fine," Michael said. "But I prefer the fresh air of the country, and of course all the exploration."

"Wait," Sharona said, turning to Everani. "What is the wandering water?"

"It's a stream. It changes its course all the time," the girl said.

"That's just an old wives' tale," Butri said. "People just can't remember the river well enough, and think it changes. They're just looking at different spots."

"No, it really does change. I've seen it." Everani stood leaned toward her brother.

"Oh yeah? When?"

"This spring! It used to go around a tree in a certain way. To the... north." The older boy scoffed, but the girl kept on. "That's right! This spring I went to the tree and it was curling around the other side!"

Butri rolled his eyes. "You just aren't remembering right. Waterways only change courses when you dig them out, or over many years. Not in a season, especially a full creek."

"I'm telling you, it changed," Everani said emphatically. "I carved my name in the tree, and now the name is facing the water. Last year it was facing the field."

Jusio laughed. "You're so stubborn. The wandering water is just a name. Just a dumb story kids tell each other. You probably couldn't remember *where* you carved your name."

The girl crossed her arms in frustration.

"I believe you," Sharona said. "Perhaps you could show me your tree sometime?"

The girl tilted her head, still pouting. "I could. Not tonight, though."

"Why is that?"

"The Glowers," Jusio said. "They come out at night. And those *are* real."

"No they're not," Butri said.

"Yes, they are," Everani said.

"What are they?" Michael asked.

"Nobody knows," said Jusio. "They're like... spirits, maybe. You can't touch them, but you can see them, but they look like a walking pile of blurry mist, like your eyes are unfocused."

"You're just seeing fireflies and swamp lights," Butri said. "Really, *you* of all people spinning yarns for a noblewoman. You're all lucky her bodyguard there doesn't slap you for trying to scare her. Really, madam, there is nothing of special interest here, except maybe my mum's cooking."

Michael laughed as he caught Sharona's eye. "The cooking *is* excellent," he said.

*

Michael followed Angelico up over the hill, and at its crest they could see what was sure to be the tree the little girl had spoken of. It stood out among all the others in the hills, for it was larger in every sense, and of an odd shape that was not quite a hardwood, like the live oaks that dotted the plain, and not like a cedar, which grew in groves to their north. Beside it ran a clear, gentle stream with green rushes along its banks.

As they got nearer, having to ford the stream to reach the tree, Michael saw that its trunk was more massive than they had originally thought. It was made to look deceptively small by its thick and heavy branches, each full of leaves that were short and flat, like something between a cedar needle and a true leaf. Michael dismounted and walked around it, touching the twisting bark and large ridges of ancient grain.

"What sort of tree is this, sir?" Angelico said. He reached up from his horse and plucked a strange green berry from a bough. He put it in his mouth to taste it.

"Be careful, the seed is poisonous," Sharona said. "As are the leaves and bark. Notice that nothing grows under this tree."

Angelico nodded and spat the berry out. "Unripe and sour anyway."

"I've never seen a tree like this," Michael said. He found the spot that held the girl's name – Everani – in thin jagged letters. The stream ran on the other side of the tree, a few feet down from the high tuffet that encased its massive roots.

"It's called a Needle Ash," Sharona said. "It grows best in the colder climbs of the petty kingdoms and even better in the North-march. There are many in the Dobo Wold, but this is the first one I have seen in the divine strand."

"Look, my prince," Angelico said, pointing to a hole in the tree bark. Michael looked into it and saw that the center of the tree was not just hollow, but missing, with rotten bark littering the floor of a tiny room within that had as its ceiling a net of branches.

"I see no sign of the stream changing course, Highness," Guissali said. He was walking between the stream and a bare patch of higher ground on the other side of the tree.

"You wouldn't," Sharona said. "This is a thin place. This tree is a memory, left behind, of where the assassins went. I'm quite sure of it, now that I look at it. Can you feel it? It… almost glows, with these yellowish leaves." Her eyes were unfocused as she looked up into the branches. "If the stream were to change course, it would be as if it had always run in the new place. That is the nature of the eternal dream which you do not understand."

"The Fay, you mean," Angelico said.

Sharona nodded. "Yes. Well, sort of. The nature of the world can be changed by those in it. Or at least, it was more changeable in the past. That schism of a realm the dark elves went into… I'm assuming it is less mundane than this one, so things may change shape or placement around the tree, just like in the other realm. The Prim may still flow there like it once did here."

"Strange," Michael said.

"To us, yes, it would be, but not to them."

"If everything is changing where it is all the time, do these… whatever they are in there, find themselves perpetually lost?" Guissali said.

Sharona cocked her head. "Not if they are like the Fay Folk."

"Fay Folk?" Michael said. "You mean the fairies? I thought these assassins were elves."

"They are like and not alike," Sharona said. "The people of the Fay are like souls waiting to be born, in tune with their own world of change. They are not lost, for there is nowhere in particular to go or to return to. The old people, those we call the elves of darkness, are still corporeal. If they have the ability to reform their world, it must be more limited. Likely they are better at navigating and adjusting to such intransigence."

"Like I said, strange," Michael said. "Well, how do we get in?"

"I don't know," Sharona said.

"What? You said that you could get in."

"No, I didn't. I said that I was capable of it, which I am. I need to learn a spell to call to them, so that we can speak to them here in this world, or perhaps one of the old spells, for bringing realms close together."

"Learn a spell?" Guissali said. "Pardon me, Lady, but how in blazes are you going to learn a spell out here?"

"Through careful thought and understanding," Sharona said. "A person's command of magic is the result of their understanding the nature of things at their core, dear Guissali. Understanding comes from study in the flesh, not just books."

"Why would they speak to us?" Michael said.

"Curiosity, or perhaps because the spell binds them to. Whatever it is, there has *got* to be a way. The assassins would not have done what they did at random. Somebody had to hire them."

"Right. Would it have to be a mage, though?" Guissali said.

"I think so," Sharona said. "Yes, I would say certainly a mage is necessary to bridge the divide, however it was done. It would take one of great power to move into that realm in corporeal form."

"Well, we have that mage in custody," Michael said. "Maybe he can reveal how he did it."

"That old nut won't crack," Angelico said. "And I doubt he will sell out any other conspirators. I wonder how he got out here and back again."

"Maybe he never came out here," Sharona said. "It could have been any powerful mage." She raised an eyebrow at Michael.

Angelico snapped his fingers. "Have you considered that the queen did it, sir?" Angelico said. "She was here, after all. I don't know when Towler would have managed coming out here, but now we know of one mage who was here just recently."

Michael shook his head. "She would have little reason to assassinate the king only after she had signed away territory to end the war."

"But perhaps not *no* reason," Sharona said. "Undoubtedly she *could* have called the assassins."

"If hostilities had broken out, she could have negotiated a better deal," Angelico said. He thought for a moment and shook his head. "That's a terrible loss of life for so little, though."

"It could still have been Towler who betrayed us in the last battle, even if another contacted these dark elves," Michael said. He sighed. "I might have been mistaken. This… I don't understand it, now."

"Should I send a messenger to your brother, sir?" Angelico said. "I mean, the king. He *is* king now."

"He is not king yet," Michael said. "But he is the monarch. He will be crowned when my father's bones and ashes are laid to rest, at home in Artalland. But don't send a messenger just yet."

"I think he would want to know, sir, that the queen may be suspected."

"Johan will want answers. I have none, yet."

"But he may meet with the queen," Guissali said. "I agree with Angelico, your highness. He needs forewarning of our suspicions."

Michael shook his head and ran his hand along the gnarled bark of the tree. "No. I know my brother, and I have learned recent lessons well. Suspicions are not enough. He will want to know for sure. Besides, Johan, for whatever I might fault him, is a shrewd man when it comes to politics. He likely already suspects the queen, if there is anything *to* suspect."

*

The night was bright, the plains and sparse trees lit by a moon nearing full. Michael sat with Guissali and Sharona in the deep, black shade of an oak tree perched on a steep slope of one of the taller hills outside the village of Havara. From their shadows they espied, at the bottom of the hill, the needle ash with its little brook running beside it. The night air was filled with the sounds of hidden life - beetles clacked and buzzed, crickets chirped, and owls called to each other. The three companions spoke little, anxiously awaiting the deepening of the night and the revelation that would mark the truth in little Everani's tale.

The stars crawled across the sky, and Sharona took out her pipe to smoke. Watching her light the bowl with a flick of magic fire from her finger, Guissali and Michael produced their own briarwood pipes, each suited to his tastes. Guissali's bowl was large and unadorned; the polish, apparent when he put fire to the tobacco, was from long years of use, the oils of his skin imparting it a dull luster. Michael's pipe was, in contrast, small and ornately carved of abstract designs, with a long stem like the one he had given to Sharona.

Michael watched Sharona's eyes glow orange as she drew on the old herb, and he perceived in her glassy stare a familiar detachment. The eyes, dark and brooding, reminded him of his father's.

"Tell me about your homeland," Michael said softly, still watching the distant tree.

"It's the same as yours," Guissali said.

Sharona didn't break her stare, but her face softened and she spoke with a quiet air. "The woods are rich. Full of trees like this one, but of lesser size and power. The fields, if you can keep them clear, are generous, give wheat and oat, even smoking leaf, in bounty for those who tend them. The people are kind and thoughtful, but like all people they have their flaws." She blew out a ring of smoke. "Too peaceful for their own good, the people of the Dobo Wold will give even a scoundrel the benefit of the doubt. But seldom do scoundrels tread there."

"I've heard tales of that forest," Guissali said. "That the trees spring to life on you."

"All trees are alive," Sharona said.

"You know what I mean," Guissali said. "They reach out and grab you."

"Only if they are told to do so, and who would do the telling?" Sharona said. "But 'tis true that we seldom get anyone in the Wold who thinks it mundane. It's a forgetful forest, and will not remember a path if there is not a man there to remember it."

"That is an advantageous defense," Guissali said. "If only we could do that for the woods of Artalland."

"Artalland is too real for that. The Dobo Wold has become too real for it, too, in the last few centuries. The more men come and go, the more mundane it becomes, and it already had precious little of the Prim left in it."

Michael took his pipe out and chewed his tongue. "My mother used to tell me… Things that might be considered heresy now." He glanced at Guissali, who had no reaction. "That there remains still pockets of the Prim in the world, where the mists of creation have not departed, like puddles on the road after a rain, before the water drains away. Not like the Fay Lands – places out in the regular world. Is the Dobo Wold such a place?"

Sharona turned to Michael at last and gave him a weak smile. "Maybe once. Now it is more a memory of the Prim. As you say, the Fay Lands still hold a piece of that first dream, the eternal dream, but they are more dangerous by far than the Wold."

"You said you'd been there," Michael said. "Once, you told me that, anyway, but I didn't really listen."

"Of course you didn't listen," Sharona said with a slight smile. "Yes, I went there once. I only wanted to go the edge, but I got lost for a while."

"Why did you go?"

"I don't remember. I presume there is a reason, though."

"What do you mean, you don't remember?" Guissali said. "It's quite a journey, going that far north."

"Oh, I remember going there just fine. I just don't remember why I went there. I do know why I left, though."

"You're such a puzzle," Michael said.

"No, I am a woman," Sharona said.

"Yes, sire, 'puzzle' doesn't begin to describe a woman!" Guissali said with a laugh. Michael chuckled with him, but Sharona did not react. Instead, she turned back to face the needle ash and pointed.

17

There was a light moving by the tree, along the water's edge. It soon faded.

"Most fascinating," Guissali said.

"That, I declare, was not light from the marsh," Michael said. "That must have been one of - what did they call them? Glowers?"

"Where did it go, then?" Guissali said.

"I think I am beginning to understand," said Sharona. "Let us get a bit closer."

"Is it safe?" Michael said.

"Nothing is ever safe, Michael," Sharona said. "But don't worry. I will protect you."

Sharona stood up and walked slowly down the hill, the wind picking up her skirt and hair. Her pipe (apparently snuffed by magic), she put away into a bag at her hip. Michael quickly got up to follow, leaving Guissali sitting alone, still smoking.

When they got closer to the tree, Michael realized that there was a mist surrounding them, very thin and pale, that barely blurred the stars and the moon above them. Sharona stopped by the stream and gave Michael a wide smile.

"Do you feel it?" she said.

Michael shook his head. "I… I see-"

"Then look," she said, and put her hand lightly under Michael's chin. She turned his face upward, where he saw, as if refracted through the mist, branches and thin, long leaves from other trees, surrounding them a few yards away in all directions.

"Where are we?"

"We're still in Midgard, but we can see it. The realm… it's like an echo." She laughed softly. "It's beautiful, isn't it? Do you remember now?"

"What?" Michael said. But even as he spoke he saw in the mist more trees, and within the trees, or between them, were buildings of strange design. Every surface, it seemed, was carved with some twisting of careful lines, and though the image was dim, it was beautiful to behold. As he looked, he could even perceive people moving, dim but clear of form, unlike the earlier shade. They were lithe and wore long hair, along with clothing of simple design, but clearly well-made. Always their eyes were obscured, glowing brightly of their own accord.

"Can they see us?" Michael said. He looked over to see Sharona almost glassy-eyed again, her lips moving silently.

"What are you looking at sire?" Guissali said, creeping up beside them.

"This… whatever this is. A vision of a village, or maybe a city."

"I don't ken, sire."

Frustrated, Michael pulled Guissali closer. "There! Do you see it? Do you see her? That maiden, watering with an open pot, by that strange stone house without doors? Do you see her strange ears, and her eyes?"

"All I see around us is a white mist, sire." Guissali squinted. "Wait. I think I see the mist moving."

"You don't have the right mind for this, Guissali," Sharona said. "I forgive you your practicality."

"Yes, but can they see *us*?" Michael continued. "Can we communicate with them?"

"Those are two different questions," Sharona said.

"Well… Pick one to answer."

"I assume they cannot see us, or they would react."

"I guess that answers the second question."

"Not entirely," Sharona said. "I have an idea. Do you have an object that you don't mind parting with? Something somebody would want to pick up?"

"Sure. How about a coin?"

Michael reached into his jacket pocket and took out a silver coin. He handed it to Sharona, who walked around the tree to where it opened to its hollow center. She dropped the coin into it.

"Nothing happened," Guissali said.

Sharona looked at him, her face nearly blank. "I am seeing if one of these people will pick it up."

"How would they if they don't know it's there?" Michael said.

Sharona smiled at him. "Of course." She withdrew her pipe and dug out some of the remaining pipe leaf from the bowl. From the leather bag at her hip she took out more of the rolled brown tobacco, and put both of the piles together, her palms up. Quietly, she spoke words that Michael did not understand. She then took the fresh tobacco and dropped it down the tree. She repacked the old tobacco and lit her pipe with a quick snap. The tree was soon full of smoke and, to Guissali's delight, blowing large smoke rings from its opening.

Sharona sat down and continued smoking, spreading her skirts out to shield her legs against the chill. After a few minutes, people approached. Their edges were blurry and indistinct, but through the thin mist, Michael could detect two pair of eyes that glowed and pulsed, light green in color, and long, almost drooping, ears that framed graceful, thin faces of pale white. It was a young girl, judging by her simple dress, and an older woman, perhaps her mother.

The specters approached the tree, growing in detail. The older one, strangely beautiful with her half-lidded eyes, looked into the tree and withdrew, to Michael's amazement, the silver coin, which was now slightly translucent. The little girl tapped the older one and pointed to Sharona. The elf startled and grabbed the child.

"Hullo!" Sharona said, and blew a smoke ring.

The older woman spoke quickly, but in a language Michael did not understand. They hurried away, becoming ghost-like again before blending into the mist. Michael peered into the hollow tree. He saw the tobacco smoking but did not see his coin.

"What did she say?" Guissali said. Apparently, he could see the girl and her mother when they were close.

"I haven't the faintest idea," Sharona said. "I don't speak the language of the Dark Elves."

"Well, that ought to make communication a bit difficult," Michael said.

"Yes, perhaps," Sharona said. "But I know now how it works. I know how to enter their realm."

"We just go into the tree, right?" Guissali said. He looked in the hollow. "It'll be a tight fit."

"Not quite," Sharona said. She stood up. "I have a few ideas now. How soon can we travel back to Forgoroto?"

"What?" Michael said. "But we haven't caught the assassins!"

"Not yet, no," Sharona said. "But I need a library if we are to talk to these people."

"A library?" Michael said.

"Yes. It's a place full of books," Sharona said. "The one in Forgoroto will have a book on the language, or it won't."

"What is that supposed to mean?"

Sharona sighed and looked through the mist, which was becoming slightly thinner. "I wonder if we can buy a few looking glasses from the villagers. Do you think so?"

"Uh... yes," Michael said.

"Good. Let's head to bed. I'm very tired," Sharona said, already dusting herself off and walking back up the hill to where their horses waited.

"Women be fickle creatures sir, and a great puzzle," Guissali said, giving Michael a slight frown. "And some *prefer* to be puzzles."

II: MIRRORS

ichael sat at the long, rough table, staring at his breakfast of ham and eggs and occasionally watching the dust motes at the kitchen window. At last, Sharona appeared, bright-eyed and fully dressed.

"Did I miss breakfast?" she said, looking around at the empty kitchen, the still hot stove with a trail of smoke curling from a leak in its stack, and the dirty dishes in the basin.

"The lady of the house had other chores to attend to," Michael said.

Sharona sighed and sat down beside Michael. She picked up his fork and began to eat his eggs. "So, did you find those looking glasses?" she said with a full mouth.

"Guissali and Angelico are on it."

She gave him a smile, which, with her cheeks full of food, made Michael think of a chipmunk.

"We will need to travel back soon," Michael said. "My brother will expect us."

"To Forgoroto? Good."

"How exactly will these mirrors help us find the assassins?" Michael said.

"You'll see," Sharona said. "If it works, that is. I'm fairly sure it *will* work."

"I need you to explain to me what you are doing," Michael said, "before I allow us to tarry any longer without progress on this errand."

"You consider looking into a forgotten realm full of uncanny beings a lack of progress?" Sharona said. She cut up a piece of Michael's ham and put in her mouth. "I've *heard* that princes were hard to impress."

"It was very impressive," Michael said. "The image kept me from sleep, if you must know, but time is short."

"It's not short, though. It's very long."

Michael growled and looked at the sun motes. "Always with the deflections. Never any answers."

"Answers are best witnessed, not given, if you really want to understand them."

"There you go again."

"Do you trust me, Michael?"

Michael looked at her. Her face was without expression again, her eyes fixed on his own.

"Do you trust me, Michael?" she said again.

Michael said after a moment, "You've never given me reason not to."

"Now who is deflecting?" Sharona said.

"And now you've eaten my breakfast."

"There you go again," Sharona said. "Besides, you weren't eating it." She stood up, still chewing. "Now, let's get to work. If everything goes as intended, we'll be back outside Forgoroto tomorrow, hopefully with a greater ability to pursue these assassins."

She walked out the back door of the house. With a grumble, Michael stood and belted on his sword. He stuffed the last piece of ham into his mouth and followed Sharona outside.

"We managed to collect ten mirrors, my lady," Guissali said. He gestured to the blanket upon which sat many different shapes of looking glasses, some fancy, some simple.

"Well, I only really needed two," Sharona said, kneeling down and picking up a hand mirror.

"A lady can never really have too many mirrors, can she?" Guissali said with a smile.

"Oh, I think she can," Sharona said. She looked at herself in the mirror and rearranged her hair to have a neater part down the middle. "Too many stokes vanity. You will be gazing at yourself, rather than life, as my mother would say. But, as long as we have more, I can make use of them."

"What do you intend to do with them, lady Sharona?" Guissali said. "Will you enchant them somehow?"

"Lady Sharona… I like that." She smiled and turned from her reflection to regard Guissali. "Yes, I'm going to enchant them. I'm going to turn them into windows. It's rather difficult to explain, but the spell work ought to be simple."

"I'm afraid I don't follow," Guissali.

"Don't worry, it will become apparent."

Michael grunted from where he stood behind Sharona. "Don't bother asking. You won't get a straight answer out of her."

"Pardon me, my prince, but you are young, and you do not yet know the ways of womankind," Guissali said. "Women never give a straight answer. You must learn to correctly interpret the answers they do give, as is their desire. This is how they test the cleverness of a man, and cleverness is very important to women. Much more so than honor."

"Don't listen to that rubbish, Michael," Sharona said. "These two ought to do." She picked out two ornate hand mirrors, both with silver handles. She softly intonated a few words, which Michael did not understand, and she passed her hands over both mirrors. She held them up and handed one to Michael.

He looked into it and at his reflection, but alongside his familiar face thought he could see, dimly, another image. He realized after a moment it was Sharona in the mirror, her face slightly-off color and almost luminescent.

"Remarkable," he said, touching the glass lightly.

"Well, it could be a bit better, but it's a proof of concept."

Michael held the mirror closer and thought he could, just barely, hear Sharona's words coming from the mirror.

"My word, Lady Sharona!" Guissali said. "This is a mighty invention indeed. We could use these to communicate while far afield without need of drums or flags."

"Don't get too excited," Sharona said, carefully stacking the other mirrors. "Magic tethers don't last very long in the World That Is. They fade with time and distance, and a connection such as this, which requires a great deal of magic from me, is not likely to last long at all. So, unfortunately, this invention will be of minimal use to us here. In the realm of the dark elves, however, where magic persists indefinitely, it will be useful. I will give one mirror to the other side, and that ought to keep the magic in this one tethered. At least, for a long while." She frowned. "I think. I wish there was a way to make the speech louder, but alas, we must talk through the glass."

"I've heard of high elves having magical talismans of various sorts, some like this," Michael said. "How do theirs not fade?"

"They were not made in this world, but in Alfheim, where all things persist unchanged. We should go there sometime. I've always wanted to."

"The way is a secret, I'm told," Guissali said.

Sharona shrugged. "Let's keep the other mirrors just in case, if you don't mind."

*

Night deepened, the pale blue swath of clear sky in the west darkening to pure black as the moon gained its waxing brilliance. Angelico, somewhat perturbed that he had missed the vision of the previous night, stood beside Sharona, Michael, and a Yawning Guissali. The night was colder than the one previous, and all of them wore their cloaks drawn close about them.

Sharona stood silently for a long time, watching the tree. After dusk died, she walked down the hill to where a barely visible mist lay about the needle ash. The men followed, Angelico warry and keeping one hand on his sword. As they gathered close around the tree the vision of the previous night slowly presented itself within layers of white mist, clearer and brighter than before. The houses of stone amid great trees stood out with sharp detail, swimming in front of the eyes, though everything seemed to glow of its own power. The shades of the elves walked amongst them, or stood relaxed, seemingly unaware of their intrusion.

"I never would have thought something like this could be here," Angelico said.

"Beware," Sharona said. "Once the veil is lifted you will view life differently, and people will call you strange for it."

"Like they do you?"

Sharona looked at him with her head cocked to the side. "Am I strange?"

Angelico cleared his throat.

"He did not mean that, lady," Guissali said, frowning at Angelico. "He thinks you wise, not strange. That is what he meant."

"Right," Angelico said.

"Michael thinks I'm strange," Sharona said. "But perhaps I prefer that. Women ought to be a little enigmatic, don't you think, Guissali?"

Guissali raised an eyebrow. "Ought to be and are, I think, be two different things."

"That's one way to avoid a question. Did you learn that from Michael?" Sharona said with a chuckle. She smiled warmly at Guissali and kneeled down. She set out a pair of mirrors and once again intonated a spell softly over them. She stood up and showed them to Guissali. "Which one is the prettiest, Gui? Which one would you pick to please your wife?"

"The one in your left hand, Lady Sharona," Guissali said.

Sharona nodded and placed the mirror into the center of the tree. She backed up several paces and held up the remaining mirror. She opened her left palm and a small blue flame appeared there, which she brought in front of the mirror. The interior of the tree began to glow in the same color.

After a few minutes, two shades walked by - the same girl from the night before and her mother, carrying pewter ewers to fill at the stream. The mother paused as she saw the light in the tree. She set down her ewer and looked inside to see the glowing mirror, whose blue light danced upon her face in a striking tone of color amid the white mist. She frowned, then turned about and, looking at Sharona and the three men, called for her daughter in an echo-like voice. The girl came, and together they ran away.

"Rats," Michael said.

"Where?" Sharona said.

"Never mind."

A few more minutes passed, in which Angelico paced around the tree, looking at the village that surrounded them in awe. Sharona had seated herself on the ground below the tree and transferred her blue flame to a small stone, which she set upon the glass of the mirror. Angelico stepped back cautiously as one of the shades approached - the little girl. She looked around herself, then carefully retrieved the mirror. She gazed into it, her eyes growing bright with their own light, before stuffing it into a small bag she carried around her shoulder. She caught sight of Sharona, looked around for a moment, then waved. From a pocket sewn somewhere in her dress she withdrew a coin and dropped it into the tree before running away.

"Well, I was hoping for an adult," Sharona said, "but a fearless child will work as well." Sharona waved her hand and the fire extinguished itself. She went over to the tree and retrieved the coin. "She left us a very odd coin."

She handed the coin to Michael, and he held it up in the moonlight. It looked to be some mixture of gold and silver, paler than gold ought to be, and yet it was brilliant in its luster, with a surface like polished glass. On the coin was stamped a dragon. Michael flipped it over to see an image of a sun and a tree.

"Very interesting."

Sharona said, "You hold onto it. Now to see if the mirror works. Let's head back for a cup of tea, shall we?"

They arrived at the house to find that some of the family were still up, doing household chores, including Everani, the young girl, who was sitting at the wash basin cleaning dishes.

"I have something for you to play with tonight, when you are done," Sharona told her, revealing the mirror, which was dark and only partially reflective.

While the three men and Sharona were having tea, Everani walked in, holding the mirror.

"What did you see in it?" Sharona said.

"A beautiful girl. Younger than me. But she's not there right now."

"It works, then," Guissali said. "Marvelous."

"Did she seem friendly?" Sharona said. "I thought she was a bit afraid of me because I'm so old."

"Remember this, my prince, for never again will you hear a woman proclaim herself old," Guissali said to Michael. Sharona gave him one of her unreadable looks, then turned back to look in the mirror herself.

"She's one of the Glowers, which is to say, she's an elf, from another world that is mingled with our own. Will you hold onto that for me tonight, and see if she will talk to you? If you can understand her, that is."

"I saw her try to talk, but I think she's speaking a different language," Everani said.

"As I suspected. I will need to take that mirror with me tomorrow," Sharona said. "But if and when I return I will give you one of your own, if you want."

Everani smiled and looked at the mirror. "Okay."

"And don't bother with your brothers not believing you. There's nothing that can harm you with that mirror. It's just a window."

*

The next day they rode back across the plains, directly toward the gates of Forgoroto, where the army of Artalland was still encamped. The gates to the city were open, and soldiers from Artalland were coming and going through it in small groups unmolested. Michael got back to the camp proper and discovered that his brother was not there, but was in the city meeting with the queen and negotiating resupply for the army, the majority of which would soon be making its trek back to Artalland and its new territories.

When Michael found Sharona again, sitting in her tent at their little camp, he saw that she had the mirror out, and was talking to it and trying to initiate gestures.

"Is the mirror still working?" Michael said, sitting down beside her and looking excitedly into it. He saw a young girl, who had placed the mirror on the ground and was pointing to various objects in a strange looking house. Though the image was dim and a bit blurry, Michael could see that the walls seemed to be made of carved wood, twisting this way and that up to the roof, and that the windows had colored glass in them, though the image as a whole was a bit washed out.

"Yes," Sharona said. "But I can't get the girl to hand the mirror to an adult. I figured out her name is Enatalla. Or at least, I think that is her name. That might be the word for girl." She pointed to Michael. "Michael."

"Michael," came back a high, cheerful voice, muffled as if sounding through a curtain. She said some words neither of them understood, then disappeared from view. When she returned, she had a doll in her possession. She showed it to the mirror and hugged it.

"Maybe try some drama?" Michael said. He waved at the mirror. The girl stopped and looked at him. "Do you have those other mirrors."

"Yes, just a moment." She got up and returned with one of the plainer mirrors they had retrieved from the people of Havara.

Michael pointed at Sharona, then at the mirror. "You. Give" He whispered to Sharona, "Give me the mirror." Sharona handed it to him. "To your father," he said to the mirror.

The girl cocked her head. Michael repeated the drama, this time standing up.

The girl shook her head. She looked away for a moment, then hurried over to the mirror. The image span sickeningly. It went dark and returned to giving a dull reflection of the normal world.

"We're going to need some help with the language," Michael said. "Let's find my brother first, though."

The gate initially wanted to turn Michael, Guissali, and Sharona away (Angelico had taken back up his command as interim high-captain of the second legion, and so was indisposed for errands), for they lacked permission from the King of Artalland or the Queen of Ferralla, but once they realized who he actually was, they let all of them pass into the city.

Forgoroto was a city no less splendid than Calasora, but remarkably different. The buildings were made primarily of square cut pieces of limestone, quarried out of great hills that rose outside the walls like vast, jagged shoulders. The roofs were tile more often than anything else, with the occasional thatch roof on stables or poorer dwellings within the walls. The houses and shops all had odd, grey streaks down their fronts from years of rain staining the cut stone; the roof tiles, where color remained, were red, but in most places, the durable clay had bleached to a mild yellow-brown. The temple, a magnificent multi-tiered structure of white stone, stood apart from the castle at the center of the city, perched on its own hill with the library adjacent. Ferral, the god of fire and steel, was enshrined there in the form of a great iron-plated statue, with gilding on his long beard, hair, and the jewelry he wore.

In most mythologies, Ferral was the husband of Artifia, the goddess of artistry and craft, and they worked together to make jewelry and other precious items. As such, Ferral's temple held an altar to Artifia, and Calasora's great Citadel held Ferral in similar reverence.

Sharona espied this altar through the stone colonnades as they walked by the temple grounds, and said, "Odd that your countries should fight, when your gods are so close."

"Even a great marriage will have its rows," Michael said.

"So do the poor ones," Guissali said. "But the weakest unions are the ones with none at all."

The castle of the city was built of four great turrets that cornered a tall keep. Unlike the city wall, it's exterior was not simple flat stone, but was highly ornate, covered with stone statues, architectural designs on buttresses and around narrow plate-glass windows, and images carved into the outer doors of iron. Everywhere, banners hung displaying a hammer, the symbol of Ferral. The castle had two outer walls which were thick and filled with many rooms, making the fortress into a palace as well as a last defense.

Into this castle Michael, Guisali, and Sharona rode, shown on by valets and other servants who already knew that Johan was within. At the second set of walls, they were at last permitted to go no further. A servant agreed to carry a message to Johan that his brother had arrived, and left Sharona and Michael to wait in the shade of an awning that had a few simple chairs. Guissali, left to stand, wandered off immediately to cavort with the Ferrallese soldiers, and had a small group laughing at him within a few minutes.

"I wonder if they realize I'm engaged to the queen," Michael said, watching Guissali. "I certainly wouldn't leave my bride-to-be sitting outside on a dirty chair."

"Don't be so sure," Sharona said, watching some horses in a nearby stable.

"What?" Michael said.

"Oh, what I mean is that, like here, you have procedures, and if your servants execute those procedures... you could be leaving your future wife in an impolite position."

"I suppose you are right."

The servant returned sometime later with a letter, sealed by Johan. Michael broke it open and read his brother's familiar neat writing:

> I'm glad you are back, brother. We have discovered much about the assassins since you left. Meet me back at the camp for supper and I shall brief you. In the meanwhile, know that the queen has been extremely amenable and helpful to our cause. The ashes of our father and our friend have been enshrined and preserved in copper caskets for transport back to Calasora. Towler has been moved to the dungeon here, which is strong enough to withstand him.

-Johan

"It looks like we aren't getting an audience today," Michael said. "Though that doesn't seem to bother Gui. Shall we find that library?"

"Just a moment," Sharona said. She took the mirror out of her bag and looked at it. With a frown, she said, "It looks like we're still hidden in a drawer."

*

The library of Forgoroto was a building of immense size and ancient age, heralding an architectural approach that set it apart from the rest of the city, save for the temple that rose above it and matched its style. Its form was simple, with high arches of dark, rough stone and narrow but tall stained-glass windows. Its doors were iron-shod and, when closed, were designed to hold well against an attack from anyone lacking a serious battering ram, a signal to some of the value held within. The pillars that held aloft the high ceiling were square and made of stacked stone that appeared seamless until one laid a hand upon the face. The ceiling was not decorated with images, but adorned with a geometric pattern of crisscrossing wood strips over painted blue paneling.

The stack of books was contained in numerous shelves, their organization almost haphazard, with books growing older as one walked from the entranceway to the rear of the building. The newest books were held in a second story that wound its way around the open foyer below.

The stack was held in the care of a frail old librarian named Boreli, who was completely unhelpful when it came to finding what Sharona sought. He had a great and many-paged ledger that held a list of all the books in the stack, as well as where they (roughly) were, but this ledger contained no information as to the subject or contents of any but a few of them.

Boreli was, however, involved enough in his own affairs of wandering the stacks and checking on the scribes, that he allowed Sharona and Michael to roam freely, incurious as to who they were or why they were there.

Michael, logically, wanted to check the rows of books far away from the front door, believing that, since Dark Elves were an extremely rare form of visitor to the realm and exceedingly ancient in their origins, a person who bothered to catalog their language likely lived far in the past.

"It could still be in the newer stacks," Sharona said. "It could have been something newly scribed from an older book, maybe from another library."

They agreed to split up, and Michael spent the first part of the afternoon pulling each book out of the shelf on a row of older dusty tomes that looked to be still in good condition. He found many odd books detailing lore of the arcane and mythological, like dragons (which, he conceded, he was a fair bit more interested in since having known Sharona), the Grey Orc culture of the wastes, the history of the enigmatic Draesenith Empire beyond the Shifted Desert (by that time more than a thousand years out of date, though the book was quite pristine), and the proper way to construct pots in the imperial style. He found several books on elves, but all of them were either creative myths or focused on the culture of the distant high elves, who, though rare, were far from a strange sight in the Divine Strand.

Growing weary of the search, Michael called out, "Found it yet?"

Sharona appeared over a balcony and shook her head.

Michael sat down at a nearby table and gazed around the room, wondering if there was a faster way to operate. He called out again, "Sharona, come down here, I have an idea."

"Why don't you come up here?" she answered back.

"This is a place of study," the librarian said, having snuck up on Michael with his soft slippers and drooping robe. He stood above him scowling, his eyes beady beneath his many-wrinkled brow.

Michael sighed and trudged up the steps to the higher stack. He found Sharona quickly pulling random books out of shelves, checking titles, and putting them back. Michael also noticed that most of the books in the newer stacks had their titles on the spine, a great improvement over the blank older tomes.

"What is your idea?" Sharona said.

"Well, I was thinking," Michael said, "that if… *somebody* from this city-"

"The queen?" Sharona said.

"Keep your voice down."

"Oh," Sharona said, looking up from a book. "Yes. Sorry."

"I was thinking that if *that person* was contacting dark elf assassins, whoever she was, she might need information on their language as well."

"Yes, a good supposition," Sharona said. She touched her lips. "She… yes…"

Michael reached a hand out and stopped Sharona from pulling a book off the shelf. She looked up at him with a surprised face. He held out a finger and ran it along the top of the book, then showed his dusty fingertip to her.

"I'm not in charge of dusting here, Michael."

Michael gently let go of her hand. "If she got the book from here, and it was put back, it won't have dust on it."

"Oh," Sharona said, the idea dawning on her. "Oh, very clever, Michael. Very clever." She held up a finger and reached into the leather purse at her hip. She withdrew a small piece of white cloth and touched it to a book. It came back dirty. "Easier to see this way."

"Good. I'll borrow one from the librarian."

"I have another one," Sharona said, and dug another handkerchief out. "Why don't you start on the other side?"

Michael nodded and walked around the balcony to the dense shelves on the other side. Quickly he went through the line, touching the cloth to the top edge of each book to catch dust, working his way slowly through the cloth, turning it grey-brown. Each time he found a cleaner book he took it out and (regardless of title) looked through its contents to see if it had any dictionary of languages. The search went quickly, and soon Sharona called out to him. He rushed over to see her holding a heavy, older-looking book with a black leather cover, the gilded letters on which had long worn off.

"This is it," she said. She pushed the book into Michael's face.

"What?" he said, flinching.

"Smell it."

Michael hesitantly obeyed and detected a sweet fragrance, very slightly musky. It was familiar, and yet he could not place it.

"Smells like a perfume," Michael said.

"Do you recognize it?" she said.

Michael thought for a moment. "Maybe. It smells like a woman's perfume."

"You had it on you, just a hint of it, after the first night of negotiations."

"I did?" Michael said. "You must have a very sensitive nose."

"I do where some things are concerned. Were you with any other women that day?" Sharona said.

Michael thought for a moment. "Only you."

Sharona smirked. "Then the queen held this book."

"Which means she really *was* dealing with the dark elves," Michael said. "But why, when we just signed a treaty, and with the whole army at the gates?"

Sharona held her hands out. "I don't know, but we left your brother in her care."

*

The sun was setting. Michael and Sharona were rushing through the city as quickly as they could without drawing attention. The streets were already slowed and crowded with people leaving, having arrived from the country in preparation for a siege. On their way to the castle, Michael ran into Johan, riding down the avenue with several retainers.

"Ho brother!" he shouted, pulling up next to Johan.

Johan smiled at him. "Good to see you again."

"I'm quite happy to see you too," Michael said, his voice unable to hide his desperation. He pulled close and said as quietly as he could, "I believe the queen was in contact with the assassins."

Johan raised an eyebrow and looked over at Sharona, who stood on her horse a few yards away, gazing up at a nearby building. "Is it her suspicion?"

"Yes. Well, it is now. I have evidence, and we can probably produce more, once we can contact the dark elves."

Johan sighed. He spoke quietly, but with a terse tone. "Michael. You shouldn't listen to that mage of yours."

"Why not?"

"She's clearly very jealous of you, Michael. She knows you will marry the queen?"

"Well... yes," Michael said. "But she knows-"

"Yes, she knows," Johan said. "How naive can you be?"

"We have evidence, Johan!" Michael hissed.

"And I will entertain it, but you should be more critical. We'll talk more of this at camp. We have found our own leads while you were away. I'll send for you once I settle some things."

Johan pushed his horse faster, and Michael lagged behind. Sharona moved over to him.

"Well?" she said.

"He doesn't believe me. But don't worry. He will. He has to."

*

Sharona held the book in her lap, turning quickly through the pages. It was illuminated in the failing light by a lamp hanging from the tree she sat under, which she had lit with her blue fire. The mirror was out beside her, dimly displaying an empty room. Michael came and sat down beside her, handing her a bowl of hot stew.

She blew on it and began eating, flipping through the book with one hand and writing on a spare page with a pencil.

"Did you find what you were looking for?"

"I'm slowly finding it, yes," Sharona said. "This is a very well-researched book. I'm trying to find the words I want. Not really bothering with grammar too much. I figure if we keep it simple we can learn what we want."

"Good idea. I want to find those assassins, but..." Michael ate a bite of his food.

"But now that you have a good idea of who hired them, it's not as important."

"Yes, that's it," Michael said. "Again, I wonder why she did it."

Sharona shrugged. "If she's nasty enough, and crafty enough, to do all this… who knows what plot she's hatching up?"

Michael nodded. "I'm going… to go talk to Langelo for a moment, and see what happened while we were away."

"Wait," Sharona said, putting her hand on his leg. "Here." She pointed to the mirror, which was moving. The face of the little girl reappeared. She smiled and waved.

Sharona picked up her scratch paper and read an odd-sounding sentence to Enatalla The girl shook her head and said something back. Sharona repeated what she had said, more emphatically, then added a word. She said aside to Michael, "That means 'it's important.'"

The girl turned away and seemed to pout. Sharona read something else to her.

"I told her I would give the mirror to another girl she could talk to, later, if she gives the mirror to her mother or father."

Finally, Enatalla turned back and picked up the mirror. Michael and Sharona had an odd view of the house and it's carved walls as they were carried into another room. They heard voices, then saw the visage of the mother, a woman with a thin face and small jaw, large ears, and eyes that glowed a soft yellow below her black hair. She looked youthful, on the edge of womanhood and not old enough to have a daughter.

"At last, an adult," Michael said. "Of sorts."

Sharona read another line to her, but midway through the sentence, the woman on the other side spoke.

"Human," said the elf. "You human."

"Yes, we're human," Michael said. "You can understand us?"

The elf turned her head in puzzlement.

Sharona spoke. "You know our words?"

"Some."

"Does anyone know more words?"

The elf nodded. "Elosha'a Shadathal."

"Can you take the mirror to - to Elosha'a?" Sharona said.

"Shadathal," the elf said. "Why?"

"We need to know… Did anyone there speak… to a human woman."

"Yes. Shadathal will know. I will take you to Shadathal."

The elf woman put down the mirror, giving them a view of a wooden ceiling containing many crisscrossed beams, and an ornate silver lamp glowing of a light that was not fire.

"Soon. You must wait," they heard her muffled voice say.

Michael waited a moment and said, "Our luck is finally turning around."

"Your Highness!"

Michael looked up and saw Langelo, who was jogging in from the camp proper.

"My brother has sent for me?"

"Yes… How did you know?"

"It's getting late and I was expecting it." He turned to Sharona. "Let's go. Bring the mirror."

"Michael," she said, holding him back with a hand on his shoulder. Her eyebrows were stitched in confusion and worry. "I have a bad feeling."

"About what?" Michael said. "We finally have the means to prove who is at the heart of the conspiracy."

"I just… I just… I don't know. I have an anxious feeling, like there's something I'm supposed to remember but can't think what it is. Something familiar and forgotten."

"It's been a long day. I'm sure it's nothing. Let's go."

III: THE IMAGE SHATTERS

The guard at the command tent, who stood with the new mage general, Morolo, was a young sergeant Michael knew from his own legion, a man named Huff.

"Sorry, highness, but this meeting is for you and the king only, per his orders," he said. Michael noticed the man's hand on the hilt of his sword. He looked over to Morolo, who stood tall and plain-faced.

"Stay here, Sharona," Michael said. "And give me the mirror."

Sharona shook her head, her eyes wide as if alarmed. "No. We can go in and show him together... then I can leave."

"Just give me the mirror and I'll show Johan. You'll be fine here. Nothing's going to happen to you protected by an entire army."

"It's not me I'm afraid for," Sharona said sternly. She clutched the mirror to her chest.

"What's gotten into you?" Michael said, stepping away from the command tent a few paces.

"It's the same feeling. Like waking up from a dream, and you can't remember the details, but you knew you had a dream. There's something here I'm supposed to do..." She turned away from Michael. "But what? What is it? Why can't I remember the dream?"

"You're acting mad," Michael said. "Well, madder than usual. Would you just give me the mirror, please? You can trust me, I won't do anything to it, and neither will Johan. He needs to see. He needs to know."

Sharona looked into his eyes, and Michael watched hers for a few seconds, which were wet and trembling. Tentatively, with shaking hands, she gave Michael the mirror. Michael smiled and nodded as he took it.

"There," he said. "I'll be right back. I promise."

He went back to the command tent, forced another smile to Sharona, and went inside.

His brother was there waiting for him, sitting at the large table with stacks of paper surrounding him.

"You summoned me, Johan."

"I am your king," Johan said, looking up.

"Not yet. You know that."

Johan chuckled softly. "True. But do you hold me as such?"

"Of course."

"Good to hear." Johan added absent-mindedly, "I suppose we shall soon know, though."

Michael approached. "I have uncovered evidence that Queen Alanrae has created or at least participated in the conspiracy to kill our father and your future father-in-law."

Johan had a strange, empty look on his face as he said, "General Butler."

"Yes. Queen Alanrae traveled to, or communicated with, the realm where the assassins came from. They are dark elves, and their world, if you wish to call it that, is here but separate and hidden, which allowed them to infiltrate our lines and escape without a trace."

"Are you sure they were not mages?"

"They might be mages in addition to what they are, but I got a very good look at them… sire. They were not human."

Johan stood up and paced slowly by the table. "What about Towler?"

"I… don't think I have been wrong about him. Someone did betray us at the battle, I am certain."

"And what evidence do you have of Queen Alanrae's part in this conspiracy?"

"First, we had testimony that she visited the village of Havara, where lies a needle ash."

"A tree?"

"A special tree. It exists both here and in the realm of the dark elves, and through that connection you can move objects, or perhaps people, between worlds."

"And you know people can be moved?"

"I believe they can be moved."

"You don't know."

Michael shook his head slowly. "I do not *know*. I do know objects can move between realms there, and that we, that is the dark elves and my party, could see each other in the vicinity."

"A good queen may visit many parts of her kingdom, just as I will visit many parts of mine."

"But under the circumstances, it is suspicious."

"I cannot act on suspicions alone, Michael."

"I know. That is why we sent an enchanted mirror to the other side, which would allow us to talk to whoever possessed it. Here it is." Michael put the mirror down on the table. It reflected the candlelight dimly.

"Hello?" Johan said, raising an eyebrow at the mirror. "It merely looks like a dark, poorly made looking glass. Are you sure it talks?"

"It needs to be held by someone on the other side," Michael said, picking up the mirror. We were waiting for… for the woman to bring it to somebody else. Shadathal."

"I should know this name?"

"No, but the mirror must still be in transport. In a bag, or the like. We'll be able to see more in it at some point. Somebody who speaks Common Mid-Verbeian."

"Have you seen one of these dark elves?"

"I have. Not half an hour ago."

"Interesting. Still, you must understand, Michael, that I cannot be-"

"There's more," Michael said desperately. "The queen's perfume. It was on a book detailing the dark elven language."

"Her perfume." Johan rubbed his forehead. "Now the queen puts her perfume on a book?"

"It rubbed off from being held, just like her perfume rubbed off on me when I kissed her hand."

Johan stood staring at him, his mouth drawn tight. "I don't remember her ever wearing perfume." He clasped his hands behind his back. "I think I understand what is happening, though."

"What? That I'm trying to protect you?"

Johan shook his head. "No. You are being manipulated."

"What?" Michael shook his head and frowned.

"That mage of yours."

"What about her? I trust her. So should you."

"Why do you think I sent her away?"

Michael felt suddenly on the defensive, seeing his brother look at him with his calm, dark eyes. "You sent her away because she helped me at the battle. Just like Angelico."

"Angelico was discharged for insubordinate speech... but I was hasty with him. I was wrong, but I didn't discharge him or any of your officers because they fought for you so bravely. I discharged them because they practically threatened a mutiny. They demanded you be reinstated, or they would resign and take their knights home with them. Father likely would have come around in a day, but such actions harden his heart.

"But your mage – she was discharged because she spoke dangerously about you. Said she had dreamt of you for years. Towler told me. She was obsessed with you, trying everything she could to be stationed near you, to talk to you. We took the appropriate action. I have a duty to protect my blood, Michael."

"Maybe she's a bit odd," Michael said slowly. "But she's brilliant and loyal-"

"She's loyal to her desire for you! Do you not see that she's infatuated with you? That she's trying to possess you for her own?"

"That's not possible."

"I told you not to be naive, Michael, but that, it seems, will always be your flaw. You trust too willingly. You believe too quickly. This woman has been manipulating you, to make you believe that your betrothed, nothing less than the Queen of Ferralla, is evil and murderous. She is sabotaging peace and a future family of great strength for her own wicked desires."

Michael shook his head and sighed. "No, brother. The evidence is clear."

"Clear as this mirror? Tell me, Michael, have you seen this mirror reveal anything outside of her presence?"

Michael thought for a few seconds. "No, but others have seen images in it."

"That's not what I asked. Tell me this, do you - do *you* - remember what the queen's perfume smelled like?"

"No, it was Sharona who smelled it," Michael said. He felt suddenly confused.

"Who did you think the traitor was? Honestly."

"Towler."

"Did Sharona start suggesting it was Alanrae?"

Michael thought for a moment. "No," Michael said. "Or perhaps she did. Angelico picked up on her insinuation and-"

"Do you see now?" Johan said. "I didn't believe her capable of this level of manipulation, or I would have had her disposed of before now."

"What do you mean disposed of?" Michael said. He felt a sudden rush of blood to his face. "What do you mean before now!?"

Johan turned his chin up, grim-faced. "I have to protect my brother."

Michael turned to run toward the door, but Morolo and Huff were there, and the sergeant had his sword already drawn.

"Is it done?" Johan said.

"Yes, sire," Morolo said.

"What did you do?" Michael said. He put his hand on his sword and his right foot forward, ready to strike with his draw.

"Don't worry about her," Johan said. "She cannot control you anymore. That is what matters."

Into the tent burst another soldier, sweaty and heaving.

"What is it?" Huff said, not taking his eyes off of Michael or his hand off of his sword hilt.

The soldier took a big breath. "We found them, sir, just where you said. If we act quickly…"

"Excellent," Johan said. Despite his brother's fighting stance, he approached and laid a hand on his shoulder. "We have been at work, Michael. The queen assisted Morolo in devising a way to track these mages, who are experts at illusion magic. Apparently it leaves traces behind, which another mage can detect, and we have finally picked up their trail." Johan looked at the soldier. "They were heading to village Lasheri, then, as I thought?"

"Yes, sire," the soldier said.

"See, Michael?" Johan said. "They were from Structania, to which they now flee."

"Trying to disrupt the peace process, sire?" Morolo said.

"Countries exhausted by war are good targets for conquest," Johan said. "Let us go, then, and meet the bastards. I want to take this blood myself." Johan walked back to the end of the table and began belting on a sword. "Will you come with me to kill these assassins, Michael?"

Michael was still frozen in his fighting stance, but the tension around him had seemed to dissolve. Was Sharona really controlling him, manipulating him, this whole time? He looked at the mirror on the table, which shined as any common one would. Of course, *he* had been the one to say that the queen had no reason to kill the king… but Structania was ruled by an old and historically ambitious family. They would have every reason to disrupt peace... Michael thought of Sharona, and her strange face, and her refusal to leave him. She was upset whenever he mentioned Alanrae… of course! How could he be so naive?

"Yes, I'll go, my crown prince," Michael said, his voice trembling. "I too desire the reckoning, for our father and for our general, loyal to the last."

"Good," Johan said. "Is your horse ready?"

"Calot is well-rested, and the best of the best. But what about armor?"

"No use against a mage anyway," Johan said. "Besides, the steel *I* need is the killing steel." He patted the pommel of his sword.

Michael nodded, and Johan followed Huff, Morolo, and the tired soldier out into the night. Michael hesitated a moment, then grabbed the mirror off of the table, compelled by a strange pang as he saw it lying dimly and alone.

Michael looked around, but he saw no Sharona and no sign of struggle. *Maybe she slipped away. She's clever,* he thought, surprised at himself for wishing her to be free and unharmed. He felt a small tug on his heart of worry, but pushed it away. The moment was a whirl of things he didn't need to feel, besides but one emotion – hatred for his father's murderers. He focused on it as he ran toward his horse.

*

Michael and Johan, along with an elite group of soldiers, rode into the wind, heading south toward the village of Lasheri, which was at the edge of the plain, two days' walk or more from Forgoroto, but still distant from the border with the kingdom of Structania. The moon was high and full, illuminating their horses as they galloped over the endless grass.

Michael felt an odd sense about the ride. It felt good, in a way, to be atop Calot with an eye for battle, but the expedition still seemed strange and uncanny, like he was riding into a dream. He could compare little else to the feeling. His thoughts strayed to Sharona and the fearful looks she gave him just hours prior, the fear she held in her dark eyes.

She was merely afraid of being found out, he told himself. *She knew Johan was always the danger to her plans.* And yet he felt sad thinking of those dark eyes, which seemed to hold such sorrow and wisdom. *A fool's wisdom.*

After midnight the party, made up of Michael, Johan, Morolo, a group of mounted battlemages, and a mixed elite cavalry troop, was spread out in a wide line. They slowed as they approached a tree-lined river. Drooping willows and hemlocks swayed in the wind as they came near, and Johan called a break to water and rest the horses for the final push to Lasheri.

Michael slowed Calot to a walk, patting the beast's heaving neck, while he watched the stars, bright and clear. The wind calmed down, and without it rushing in his ears, and without the pounding of hooves, Michael could hear at last the men around him talking to each other. As he entered the deep shade of the willow trees, he noticed something. The leaves and drooping branches around him were lit softly from below. He looked around and realized he was all alone, though he could hear still the other knights.

He saw after a moment the source of the light: his saddlebag. Twisting around, he opened it and pulled out the mirror, which he had for a weak moment been loath to leave behind. It was, in the deep dark under the trees, glowing brightly with an image of several dark elves, all talking in their strange language.

"Hello?" Michael said, casting a glance around. About thirty yards away he could see two knights that were dismounted and leading their horses to a wide, moonlit stream.

"I see you now," said an elf sitting close to the mirror. His features were sharp and pronounced, with a high prominent brow ridge and long ears. His face was unbearded, and his jaw, though slighter than a man's, was square.

"Are you real?" Michael said. "Shadathal?"

The elf laughed and looked to another sitting near at hand. Michael could see they sat in ornate chairs of carved beech wood, and were in a stone building of some sort. "Yes. Should we not ask you the same thing? Are you real, or merely a clever a bit of magic?"

"I thought... " Michael said, trailing off. *Sharona isn't here. She can't be enchanting this mirror. This is all real. So what about the queen? Is that real too?*

"I was told this was important, not merely a bauble for our amusement."

"Yes," Michael said, turning back to the mirror. "Sorry. I have much to consider right now that I should not be distracted by. Three nights past two of your people assassinated two men." Michael watched the face of the elf go slack. "They escaped back into your realm. I sought them, for…"

"To exact your revenge?" Shadathal said.

Michael hesitated. "To bring justice."

Shadathal looked to the other elves around him, two males looking to be of equal stature and age. They talked quickly in their language. Shadathal turned back. "What else do you have to add?"

Michael thought for a moment. "Did you see a woman, a human woman, who either passed into your realm or else talked to you the way we are now? Her name was Alanrae."

The elves talked for a moment. Shadathal said, "We do not aim to meddle in human affairs."

"You meddled when your assassins killed my… my king."

"We ordered none to do this," Shadathal said, his eyes curiously looked to his companions. "But we know who might have. We will deal with this affair on our own, with our own justice for such acts."

Michael breathed quickly. Beneath him, Calot moved, sensing the tension in his heels. "Can you tell me about the woman, for our own justice? I believe she hired these assassins. If not, who did? Whoever did so would have to have appeared in your realm in some form."

"Describe the woman," Shadathal said.

"She has long, dark hair that curls, and wears fine dresses. Her eyes are blue. She's very beautiful, and a powerful mage."

"I know this woman. She is not known as Alanrae here. She has not shown herself in our village for some time, but may have gone to other places in our realm. Does that satisfy you?" Shadathal said.

Michael hesitated. "Tell me one more thing. Did she wear perfume?"

Shadathal chuckled. "Yes, actually. She smelled like a stag's sex glands." The elves near at hand chuckled. "We have remarked over it in the past, that humans must have dull senses to pile on and tolerate such strange stenches, though we would not say that to her face. Saying something about it would offend our own sensibilities."

"Thank you, Shadathal," Michael said. "I appreciate your candor and your honesty. These are virtues to men."

"To all free people such are virtues, though your memory of them be but an image of what once was."

"I'm going to put you away now, but can you keep the mirror near? The new king will want to see you, if you are willing."

"I suppose I am willing," Shadathal said. "This is the turn of the day in which we reflect with our friends."

"Very well… sir."

Shadathal smiled and nodded. Carefully, Michael put the mirror in his lap and rode over to where he saw the knights assembling, looking for his brother, but as he milled through the men, he could not find him.

"Johan, where are you?" Michael said. "I have something to show you. This mirror!" Michael pointed to his lap as he caught sight of his brother, who was atop his horse on the other side of the river.

"It should have been much simpler, Michael. If only you had stayed home, like you were supposed to," Johan called back. He was flanked by a number of dragoons, who had crossbows in their hands.

Michael picked up the mirror and held it up, letting the image shine outward. "I have it, Johan! They will confirm that it was the queen. I don't know who we're chasing, but it's not the true assassins." Michael looked about himself. "Where did you ford the river? Let me come over and show you."

Time seemed to slow as Michael watched the dragoons raise their crossbows and fire, a wave of bolts flying toward him. Calot reared and the volley struck the unbarded horse, thudding into his flesh like hailstones on a canvas tent. The beast did not cry out in his death-throws, but collapsed down to his knees, allowing Michael to dive off. With horror, Michael watched Calot roll over, pierced with more than a dozen bolts, and at last the horse screamed.

In a heartbeat, Michael was up, his sword drawn. The knights on his side of the river were running toward him or attempting to mount up, clearly not expecting Michael to have survived the volley of crossbow bolts. Everyone was shouting.

Why? Michael thought as he ran for the cover of the willow trees behind him, hoping to avoid another volley. *Johan is trying to kill me!*

An unhorsed knight jumped over a fallen log and brought down his longsword in a stabbing motion. Michael, lacking any other impediment, pushed the tip to his side using the back of the mirror, which he still held in his left hand. The sword slid past Michael's body and into the stump of a tree. The knight continued his forward momentum, stumbling on the stump. Michael turned the tip of his own bastard sword up. It bounced off the knight's vambrace and slid along the breastplate. The tip found purchase in the gorget, and with a sickening pop broke the mail there and slid up into flesh, biting the inside of the knight's jaw and skull. Blood poured out of the wound as Michael rolled back, allowing the knight to fall to the ground, gurgling and thrashing.

Michael leapt to his feet to face another attacker. Quickly finding his footing, he pivoted his hips and leaned forward, bringing the mirror up near his right hand as a buckler. The knight attacked and Michael quickly knocked away the blow and countered, driving his point into the man's thigh where his chausses, meant for riding, hung awkwardly to the outside of the leg. The man collapsed to one knee, and Michael leapt away, diving through branches as he felt more bolts hit trees all around him.

He could hear the pounding of hooves, but knew there was nowhere to hide. He needed to get to another horse and flee - it was his only chance. He ran for the next cluster of brush, thinking he could make the men dismount there to fight him.

"What it is going on there?" came the voice of an elf. Michael turned over the mirror to see the face of Shadathal staring back.

"I'm being attacked."

"Do you know any connection lightweaves?" the elf said.

"What?"

"Do you know linking magic? You can use the mirror to pull yourself into this realm."

"I'm not a mage." Michael ducked under a sword swing as a knight rode past. Hastily, he stabbed the horse's back leg, causing it to falter and throw the rider a few paces away, it's leg suddenly without strength.

"Not all humans can weave magic," one of the elves said.

"How did you enchant this mirror?" Shadathal said.

"I didn't!" Michael attacked the unhorsed knight even as his enemy was struggling to pull himself upright, hindered by his plate armor. Half-swording as best he could while holding the mirror, Michael thrust into the man's groin. The tip slid through mail and jack easily, and Michael jumped back to avoid a countering sword-swing, knowing the wound would keep the knight from running after him, but would still take a long time to bring death.

He was almost at the next heap of brush and fallen trees, but stopped as two mounted knights pulled in front of him, lowering their lances. Michael dropped into a fighting stance, knowing he could do nothing against the long sharp polearms, but unwilling to die.

He started and fell backward as a huge wall of dirt erupted around the horses, knocking one along with its rider down to the ground. The other horse spooked and bolted, carrying the rider with it.

Seeing the fallen knight struggling to get his horse back up, Michael attacked. The man was distracted and off-guard, his lance forgotten, but he was still quick enough to draw his own sword. Taking a forward-leaning stance again, Michael edged in on the man deflecting a few longsword blows while trying to cut again into the man's groin.

"Fire!" Michael and the knight were temporarily distracted by the order. They both paused and looked to find the dragoons on the other side of the river firing another crossbow volley, but this time the river was twenty yards or more away, and the troop still on the far side of it. They could see the mass of deadly bolts shooting towards them at immense speed.

The knight shrieked. Michael, in shock, stood silent, watching them. A bright light erupted and the bolts were suddenly on fire, falling in different directions as they burned. One struck the knight in his leg while another hit his the horse in the flank, but none seemed to find Michael.

"Quickly Michael!"

Michael turned about to see Sharona, atop Rabble-Rouser, stomp through the brush. His heart seemed to leap into his throat and drop into his bladder at the same time. She stopped the horse in front of him, her eyes searching the far river bank.

"Sharona!" Michael said. "Thank the Dreamer!" He scrambled on the back of the horse and she snapped the reins, pushing the beast through branches and mud and out into the open. Michael looked back to see more of the cavalry assembling, moving outside the ragged tree line, clearly of mixed ideas of what to do with Johan still on the other side of the river.

"We'll never outrun them with two on this horse," Michael said. "Head for that river bend. We might be able to lose them in the crossing."

"Are you hurt?" Sharona said.

"Just some scratches."

"Are you still there?" came a voice from the mirror.

"Yes," Michael said.

"Did you hear what I said about the mirror?" said Shadathal.

"Is that the mirror?" Sharona said.

"Yes," Michael said. "And no, Shadathal, I did not hear you."

The elf's muffled voice was barely audible above the pounding gallop. "I said if you can weave the right connection, you can use the mirror on this side to pull you in. I can do the correct weave on this side. "

"I can't lightweave," Sharona said to the mirror. "Whoever you are. Is there any other way?"

They both ducked as they heard the whistle of bolts being un-leashed from behind them, falling wide. Rabble-rouser pounded on, unperturbed. Michael looked off to their left and saw horsemen fording the river and charging up a gap in the bank where the trees were sparse.

"The only other way is to have an object of permanence from this realm," Shadathal said. "And to have a deep command over its nature, but that is the magic of the lesser elves."

"Damnit," Michael said. "We're going to get cut off. Head to the right there. Toward where the river dips down."

"Michael, do you still have the coin?" Sharona said, obeying Michael. "The coin the girl gave us?"

Michael reached into his pocket and felt the smooth, mirror-like surface of the large coin there. "Yes, it's here."

"I'll have to try it. Here!" She turned Rabble-rouser to the left again, galloping toward the closest trees. The sound of pounding hooves grew louder. More bolts flew - wide, again, though Michael could feel some hit the ground around the horse.

The pair ducked under some branches and Sharona reined in Rabble-Rouser.

"Quickly, give me the coin," she said, turning back.

Michael reached into his pocket and found the coin. As he handed it to Sharona, the horse bucked, frightened by a bolt of mage fire slamming into a nearby tree, bursting and charring the bark. Michael fumbled the coin and it fell into the brush below.

"Damn it, I forgot about the mages," Michael said.

"Give me the coin," Sharona said emphatically.

"I dropped it," Michael said, already sliding off the saddle and dropping into the long grass below.

Frantically, he searched through the long blades and small shrubs below the trees, but couldn't locate the coin. Sharona threw her hand out above him and turned back what looked to be a large ball of fire. It slid away into the shadows, wobbling, then burst into red fire.

"Find it, hurry!" she shouted.

"I'm trying!"

"Stand back!"

Michael jumped backward and Sharona dismounted. She raised a hand and instantly the grass in front of them leapt into blue-green flame. The grass twisted and curled as it burned in the magic fire. Amidst the flames, Michael saw a flashing of light.

"There it is," Michael said. He threw his leather-gloved hand into the flames and picked up the coin, which was burning hot. Sharona held out her hand, but Michael held back the coin. "It's too hot, wait a moment."

Michael felt a dull thud in his ribs, followed by a terrible pain, and suddenly his breath was gone. He reached to put a hand under himself as he felt his legs give way.

"Michael!" Sharona screamed. She reached into his hand and took the hot coin, crying in agony as she did so. She held tight onto Michael as she repeated strange words.

With a bloom of eerie pale green light, their surroundings blurred and began to change. The grasslands were replaced by rich trees, the willows changing to ashes and yews, the hemlocks to tall pines. Michael saw his pursuers, close at hand, fade into shades.

One knight, a few yards distant, suddenly burst back into clarity, appearing as if made of mist before becoming fully corporeal. He thrust a lance downward and Michael, summoning what strength he could, popped himself off of the ground and dodged the point, which landed just under his aching ribs and caught in the dirt. The knight abandoned it and drew his sword as he edged his horse around.

Sharona screamed in pain again, and as she did, the knight faltered, his horse bucking. Soon his screams and Sharona's were mingled, and he fell off the horse, dropping his sword and scratching at his body like a man possessed.

Michael rolled over, feeling the arrow in his ribs catch against the ground, struggle against flesh and bone, then break. The knight continued screaming and pulled his helmet off. He started scratching at his face and the jack hood he wore, tearing his skin, his voice cracking madly. Michael got to one knee and dove forward, thrusting the point of his sword at the man's neck. It landed, then after a moment of resistance, plunged inward, silencing the horrible wails. Michael collapsed again, panting, as the man writhed and then slowly became still.

"Sharona," Michael said with effort, feeling a pain so intense in the left side of his ribs and back he could barely tolerate taking a breath. "Sharona, where are you? Are you alright?"

"I'm here, Michael," she panted, crawling over to him. He saw her face above him, stained with dust and tears.

"Thank the gods." He felt her arms wrap around him, and heard her sobbing and felt her shuddering. It made his breaths hurt even worse.

"I've failed you again," she said.

"Let go, Sharona," Michael said.

"I'm sorry. I never should have-"

"Let go!" Michael cried.

She pushed herself up, then gasped as she saw the arrow wound in his ribs.

"You're hurt," she said.

"Pretty bad," Michael choked out. "I think... it got past the ribs... and... maybe not the lung, though."

"Let me see if I can get it out," Sharona said, trying to pull the cloth of his jacket away from the stub of the arrow.

"No," he said. "If you just pull it out, it'll…. break the seal of my diaphragm… I won't be able to breathe."

"You already can't breathe." Sharona began to sob again. "It's just like the dream, Dreamer help me…"

"Get… a grip. I'll… tell you what to do. Just… get me on my side."

Sharona nodded and rolled Michael onto his good side, wincing as he groaned with the pain.

"That's better," Michael said. He looked off into a wide, verdant forest. The trees, he realized, glowed with their own soft, comforting light of pale green and yellow. It felt peaceful, even through the pain.

"Just as second." Sharona pulled off her own coat and rolled it up. She placed it in the small of Michael's back. "Is that better?"

"Yes. The arrow has to come out, but something else will have to go in. At least… until we can get to a proper Nosteran Cleric. Otherwise, the barb will just work its way deeper."

"Alright," Sharona said, wiping her cheeks with the sleeves of her dress. "What do I need to do?"

"Get a firm piece of cloth, something as tightly woven as possible. Or leather from a waterskin, if you can manage."

"I have one of these cloths," she said, holding up one of the dusty handkerchiefs from the library.

"It'll do in a pinch. You have any paper to wad up in it?"

"Yes, hold on." Sharona stood up and returned with the library book, which she ripped a page from.

Michael nodded. "Wad it up and wrap it with the cloth. Try to make a nice little long log of cloth and paper. When you pull the arrow out, shove that in. That'll stop the bleeding and we'll be able to get it out later when it's time to cauterize the wound."

Sharona took a knife from her belt and cut away the jacket and Michael's shirt, revealing his bloody ribs. She grabbed the arrow and pulled, but it wouldn't budge. Michael twisted and groaned.

"Use your boot."

"Are you sure?" Sharona said.

"Do it."

Sharona stood up and put her boot on Michael's ribs by the arrow stump. She pulled up with all her might. Michael cried out, now softly, in new pain. The arrow loosened a little, and with a slow effort, it came free. A fresh rush of blood came out. She grabbed the little cloth bundle, but stopped as Michael grasped her hand and rolled forward. More blood came out, staining the green grass underneath. Michael coughed, then nodded.

Sharona pushed the cloth up against the wound, but it wouldn't go in. She rolled it tighter and tried again, pushing hard with her thumb until it went into the wound. Michael writhed a little, but didn't scream as it went in.

Michael was silent a moment. He then took a deep breath and screamed through gritted teeth. His scream faded and he took a few ragged breaths.

"So much better," he groaned.

"Really?" Sharona said. "You lost so much blood."

"The space between my ribs and lungs was filling with it. It was getting hard to breathe. I'll be better now, but we have to get the wound cleaned and closed in the next day." He rolled back on his side and put a hand out on Sharona's leg. She grasped it in both of hers and started sobbing again.

"I'm sorry, Michael."

"You saved me. Don't apologize for that." He took a hard breath. "I thought you were dead or captured."

"By whom?" Sharona said.

"Johan."

"I ran away as soon as you went in the tent. I knew right away they wanted something with me."

"Johan... It was always Johan. He convinced me so easily... How could I have doubted myself so? I'm sorry Sharona, I betrayed you."

"How, exactly, did you betray *me?*" she said.

"I betrayed you in my heart. I chose not to believe what was true. I chose... I chose to believe a man without honor, knowingly." His eyes swam as he turned his gaze to the shifting layers of glowing leaves. Michael frowned. "Someone is approaching."

Sharona picked up Michael's sword and turned, her eyes blazing and ready for a fight.

IV: The Schism

Michael saw a light approaching, not from the softly luminescent trees, or a lamp, but from many sets of eyes and glowing baubles of glass, hanging from tall elven figures or fitted on staves like magic torches. The strangers approached slowly. The men were clothed in robes or in trousers and simple shirts, the women in long dresses of single dark colors. Their hair was a variety of shades, Michael saw now, of dark brown, black, red and umber, and their eyes too were of odd shades, purple and yellow and even dull red.

"I never got your name," one of the elves said in a deep, resonating voice.

"Shadathal," Michael said, smiling. "Michael is my name. How did you find us?"

"The mirror. I followed the weaving. You may put your sword down," he said to Sharona. "If we cared to harm you we would have already done so."

"Can you help him?" Sharona said. "He's been hurt badly."

Shadathal looked impassively at Michael. "Such as we can. We will need to get him back to Elosha, where we have greater access to our healing implements."

"I will make a litter for him," a female said from Shadathal's side. She held aloft a short stick with a glowing glass ball in the middle, the wood twisted around it. The tree above croaked and groaned, and two branches dropped down. She put away the device and began to tie the ends of the branches together, then all the limbs. The green wood of the ash tree was supple and easily manipulated, and soon the branches were a litter. With a nod to the tree, the branches broke free of the trunk and the elf brought the litter forward.

Two elves joined her and they lifted Michael, placing him on the litter, prompting him to grunt and groan with the handling. While he settled himself, they attached the litter to the saddle of Rabble-Rouser.

"What shall we do with the body?" Shadathal said, nodding to the dead knight. "Was he a companion of yours, or an enemy?"

"Enemy," Sharona said, still breathing heavily. "I… I don't know your burial customs, but ours is usually to set the body in the earth, or else burn it in a pyre."

"It's only a shell," Michael croaked. "Dispose of him as you will, as we cannot take him back to his family's resting place."

"What of his armor?" said one of the elves.

"Spoils of war," Michael said with a grin. "It's yours if you want it."

"Thank you," Shadathal said. "We are poor here in things made of steel, for our minds are not in it. Afalla, please make another litter for the other beast to carry the body."

The same female as before raised her strange stick and repeated her process, pulling green limbs and making a litter for the knight's body. Soon they were off, the horses being led through a winding path, little more than a game trail, with a glowing roof of wood and leaves overhead. Michael tried to still his breathing as they moved. He felt light-headed and every bump was a pain.

Michael watched Sharona's face as she walked beside the dragging litter. It was contorted in pain, and he wanted to say something, but found himself too weak to talk. He reached a hand toward her, but she did not reach back, seeming not to notice the effort. He closed his eyes and tried to listen.

"This place is much more beautiful once you are in it," Sharona said through a pant.

"The mundane world is beautiful too," Shadathal said. "But like a painting to which many artists have contributed - chaotic and baroque."

"How did this place come to exist?" Sharona said.

"We dreamt it," Shadathal said. "And as we came to one of the last remaining dwellings of the ancient prim, it was so. Long we have labored to maintain it, as the world around crept in. Eventually, we had to seal the Prim away, to keep what we had created, or to let it grow, as you see it, and the realms were separated. We pulled up the mist realm, Niflheim, into the world that is, and so have cordoned a part off in the world where the Prim flows eternal cold, but clear enough to keep our dream alive. There are other refuges in the world, if you know where to look. I wonder how long we will hold this one."

Michael forced his eyes open, and caught Sharona looking back sadly at him, then he allowed his vision to rest.

*

Michael had fallen asleep on the trek, and woke up when they finally stopped to find Sharona and Shadathal standing still beside Rabble-Rouser, talking quietly. They were in a large cluster of buildings, some of stone, others of fine wood, and some still that were carved partly out of the trunks of great trees.

"You must care a great deal for him," Shadathal said.

"Yes, I must," Sharona said. "I *must* care for him, but… it is more. I will provide whatever you need, pay any price, if you but help him live."

"There are those in the many worlds that would take advantage of such an offer," Shadathal said. "But you have already gifted me several things. Steel armor, for if the need arises, and these mirrors, which I find novel and inspiring. You must be a powerful mage, for this magic is beyond our comprehension."

"It's a simple thing. I could make you more, if I had more mirrors. So, will you heal Michael?"

"I will. When he recovers, I may ask another favor. *Ask,*" he said. "You may refuse."

"I won't."

"It is unwise to commit to the unknown."

"Then I am unwise," Sharona said. "I have committed the unknown course that is this man… oh, how long I dreamt of him."

"You created him?"

"No," Sharona said. "I don't think so. I was given a dream… it's hard to describe. I spent a long time in a dream that is parallel to that which I live with him."

"Interesting. A dragon dream, perhaps?"

"Yes. A dragon dream."

"I will get to work on him. He will be infirmed for some turns, but it takes time for a more mundane body to be healed."

Michael laid his head back down and closed his eyes.

***

Michael woke.

His vision was hazy, but he realized he was in a bed. The ceiling above him was a lattice of tiny wood slats, almost like a basket. Lamps of glowing glass globes, magically illuminated in pale greens and blues, hung from chains. Michael turned over to see Sharona slumped beside the bed in a large, comfortable-looking chair, her hair tangled and partially covering her face. She was snoring softly, and it was clear to Michael she had not bothered to wash her face since the battle, for he detected among the grey grit of her face flecks of dried blood, probably his own, and long tracks of pale flesh made clean by the passage of tears.

He felt along his left side with his right hand, and found a bandage covering where the wound had been. He touched it, and breathed hard through his teeth at the pain.

Sharona sat up suddenly and saw him awake.

"You're awake," she said calmly, moving over to the bed and pushing her hair out of her face. Her eyes were clear and bright, their dark brown irises like mirrors, but Michael saw already tears collecting on her lower lids. She began to fix Michael's bedding as she talked. "You're awake, which means the fever has passed. You may be confused. You've been here two days, and Shadathal has been working on your wound, which was apparently from a poison bolt. I have a potion I was bidden-" Sharona paused as Michael touched her face with his hand.

"Sharona."

"What is it Michael?" she said, half choking.

"May Grim take me if I ever call another face beautiful."

The tears began to spill over Sharona's eyes and drop to the bed as she gave a nervous chuckle. "I'm… I'm not pretty." She looked around suddenly. "And I haven't washed. I'll be-"

"You are beautiful," Michael said, gripping her arm. "You are a more lovely thing than I could ever have imagined on my own. Better than a dream. And you saved me. Why did you follow me so far and so wide?"

"Because I dreamt that I would," she said. "I spent… a very long time dreaming. That you would need me. And because… because…" She took a deep breath and wiped tears from her face. "Because I love you, Michael. Because I have always loved you. *Always.*"

Michael chuckled. "Johan was right. About that one thing. He saw how you felt for me, even though I refused. Sharona, I *did* need you. The whole way. I will still need you, undoubtedly, in the time to come."

"And I will help you," she said, smiling, though the tears still slipped over her cheeks.

Michael pulled her close, tugging on the shoulder of her dress, and kissed her softly on the lips. When she sat back up, he said, "I have never considered love before. Forgive me my hardness."

"I forgive you."

Michael laughed. "The polite thing would be to profess that there is nothing to forgive."

"But that would be a lie, Michael. There is much to forgive, and I forgive it."

She ran her hand over his forehead, and Michael took it, noticing an odd feeling to it. He held her hand saw upon her palm in raised, pink flesh, the image of a dragon.

"What happened to your hand?" he said.

"The coin. It was so hot when I picked it up… but I couldn't let go."

"Of course. You were in so much pain. I'm sorry."

"I'm alright now. The elves had a salve that healed it marvelously." She gave him her usual half-smile. "Besides, it taught me something. I understand now, perfectly, what it means to have one's flesh burning. That was what I used on the knight that was attacking you."

"Batoli was his name," Michael said. "I thought him a good man, once, when he was a cavalry officer in my brother's legion."

"He might have been a good man, once."

"True. Now go get a bath and stop worrying about me. I'll be fine without you snoring next to my bed."

"I don't snore. You must have heard something else."

Michael nodded, suddenly aware that he was crying. "I must have, yes."

*

In the realm of the dark elves, day and night were not a foreign concept, but did not pass the way they did in the world that is. The light came not from a sun, but from the canopy of trees that roofed them in. Patches of sky between these branches showed stars, brighter and larger than what they should have been, along with a great dim red moon, but little else besides a slight turning to deep blue during what might be considered day by the elves. For half of each "turning," as the elves called a day, the trees would brighten and change to a golden hue, then dim to a deeper green when it was time for sleep. Time was measured fastidiously by a series of hourglasses and mechanical devices which each household would turn each day or division of time. One large contraption, powered by magic contained in vessels of water, was housed in the central meeting hall, providing a measure of time from which all could coordinate their own instruments.

Michael recovered quickly, helped by a viscous and foul-tasting potion that Shadathal produced for him each morning. He was soon able to walk without great discomfort, and within a week was able to touch the wound without doubling over in pain. Sharona was with him always, fawning over his needs in a way that Michael found a bit annoying, though he never said so.

"You are an ambitious man, Michael," Shadathal said to him early on one day, as Michael sat in the bright common garden, running a whetstone along his notched sword while Sharona perused the book on the dark elf language, writing frequently in the margins with a pencil.

Michael shook his head. "That, I am not. I'm a second son, and have always been content to be so."

"Are you sure about that?" Sharona said.

Michael shook his head. "Maybe not content, but more than willing to have my place."

"I do not speak of politics," Shadathal said. "But of your recovery. You should still be lying in bed. You were gravely wounded and poisoned."

"Well," Michael said. "I had your potions to help me."

"Certainly they countered the poison, but they should not have closed your wounds so quickly."

"There are mages who can close wounds in Midgard," Sharona said.

"I have heard," Shadathal said. "We do not mend wounds in that way here. Each person must restore himself."

"That's the natural way of things," Michael said. "The restorative properties of the body often surprise me, as a soldier."

"Sharona said you were a prince."

Michael looked over at her. She shrugged. "They were going to find out sooner or later," she said.

"Yes, I am a prince, but I was a soldier once, too. That, truthfully, is more of me than my title as prince, but I think both titles I have lost now. You see, it was my brother, the king now, I should think, that sought to slay me, and it was he who engineered my removal from command." He looked up at Shadathal. "What shall I be, then?"

"Can one man change the nature of another?" Shadathal said.

"It seems," Michael said.

"And yet you sharpen a sword."

"Just something to do," Michael said.

"I would conjecture that what we choose to do exhibits who we are."

Michael was silent for a moment, working on a dull part of the sword edge. "Batoli - the dead man near me - what did you do with his body?"

"We interred it according to the customs prescribed by Sharona," Shadathal said. "He was buried in the earth, with the place of his burial marked, and a prayer said to the Dreamer, that he might return."

"Not his god, but just as well," Michael said. "Thank you."

"I find it interesting that you show such concern for your enemies."

"You honor the dead, and the dead shall honor you. He wasn't my enemy because he was a monster, but because of who his master is. That is something about soldiery you come to understand after battle. The men you slay are never the evil, twisted things they are said to be, but are merely other soldiers serving the wrong side of things." Michael chuckled and stood up. "That at best, really."

"That sounds difficult on the… on the soul, as you would say," Shadathal said.

"It engenders a respect and admiration for the men you fight. And a soldier who does not respect his enemy will find himself surprised by the enemy's power. That respect for life, even on the field of death, is where the edge of honor lies. It is how a battle can be won without killing every last man, and how, as a commander, you know that if you must surrender, you do so to another man, with his own honor." Michael flicked out his sword tip with blinding speed, severing a flower from a hanging vine. He caught it as it fell, and handed it to Sharona. "When these things fail, that is when war is truly hard on the soul. In spite of all that is happened, I am thankful that we did not have to lay siege to Forgoroto. What would be written on the souls of my men would be horrific."

"How far have you traveled, Michael?" Sharona asked. "How far from Artalland have you been?"

"I've been to five kingdoms of the twelve of the Divine Strand."

"You are lucky, then. It is not as you say it is elsewhere."

"It is not as I say it is within my own home," Michael said. "Look to my brother."

"He is not a soldier, not a warrior," Sharona said. "He's a politician."

"That he is, or he would have managed to kill me," Michael said, chuckling.

*

Turns passed, the endless cycle of the strange realm healing Michael beyond what he thought possible. He felt stronger than before, and took to practicing with his sword. The comfortable clothing he had been given was loose and made him feel rushed and young when he went through his forms. He wished to go riding, to break in and train the horse he had acquired from Batoli (a good brown destrier which he had renamed Turner), but Shadathal cautioned him not to go far afield.

"The paths do not run always straight here. You may return along the same path and end up somewhere else, since you are not from here," Shadathal said one day, as Michael rode the horse around a gentle pond filled with koi.

"It is like that in the Dobo Wold," Sharona said. She was reclining and reading the same book she had been under the light of a tree. "I have a few spells which can help."

"All the same, I would prefer if you kept to pastures here," said the elf. "There are dangers afield that you have not yet seen or sensed. Things that even we fear, for the Prim obeys no master."

Michael practiced the horse's paces a few more times, then dismounted and left it to wander in a fenced pasture, along with several of the elves' horses (which seemed, to his eyes, quite fine, in a variety of painted colors). As he watched the horses, two familiar faces approached. Enatalla, the girl who had picked up the mirror, was approaching with the other elf maiden. Sharona greeted them in their language.

They had a short conversation, leaving Michael standing by the side. In a pause in the conversation, Sharona turned back to Michael and said, "Shadathal seems to have kept the mirrors, and Enatalla enjoyed seeing the other girl from the village. Do you think we would have another opportunity to go back there? Her mother thought I might make another mirror for her."

"That's her mother?" Michael said, looking on the still young and slight face of the taller maiden. "She doesn't look old enough."

"She's quite old," Sharona said. "Apparently she waited a few centuries longer to marry than is standard, I have gathered from speaking to her. But to her question – will we return to Havara?"

"I don't know," Michael said, smirking at the thought of the lithe elf before him being hundreds of years old. "Will we ever leave here?"

"What do you mean?" Sharona said.

"I have been thinking… I have no clear path anymore. My brother seeks my death. I will have to go into exile, into hiding. What shall I become? I consider now… perhaps we could stay here. You and me."

"Just a moment," Sharona said. She turned to the little girl and spoke, and the two elves walked away. When she looked back, there was a frown on her face.

"What?" Michael said. "It seems a far better potential for life than going back to Ferralla, or Artalland, or elsewhere, where I will have to be a mercenary to survive. A simpler life. Here."

Sharona looked around her, her eyes lingering on Shadathal's mansion of stone and living wood. "It is tempting, Michael. Do not think I haven't thought of that, or even wished it. Even now I wish it, as I imagine a life..."

"But you oppose such a decision."

"It supposes that Shadathal will even permit us to remain. But if he did, would you find enough life here?"

"There's beauty, food, peace, companionship, comfort. What else does one need?"

"The question is what *you* need. Would you be satisfied with me alone?"

Michael smiled. "Well, I expect that I would learn the language. It seems you already have. There *is* fellowship here."

"They aren't the same as us, Michael. Who would our children marry?"

"Children?" Michael said.

"Yes, or would you subject me to a life without such? Who would they marry, elves?"

"I suppose... Why not?"

Sharona grunted and put her hands on her hips. "That's not even my point."

"Well, what is your point?"

Sharona took a breath and stepped closer to Michael. "My point... Who are you?"

"You know who I am."

"Tell me."

Michael rolled his eyes and said, "I am Michael, son of Eduardo, of the house Harthino, prince of Artalland, High-captain of- wait, not that."

"Do you understand now?" Sharona said, putting her hands on his chest. She made a fist and thumped it on his breast. "The heart of you is what you just said. I don't believe you would ever be satisfied by a life of simple comfort; a life unchanging."

"So what should we do, exactly?"

"That is for you to decide. After this, things become hazy."

"What becomes hazy?"

"The dream," Sharona said. "The dream I was given, in the Fay, of you, of what I was doing with you... I can't remember much now."

"You had a dream of the future?"

"No, not exactly. I don't think so. I believe I saw a dream... of another being. Maybe the dreamer himself. He showed me a thing of potential, but it was so complex, it took so long to dream it... Like living another life. It was wonderful, living that dream with you, but now I can scarcely remember it, except snippets, when before it was so clear. Like I can only remember it when we are enacting it. Or maybe it's like the voice said…"

"The voice?"

"A dragon. One of the great dragons, gods of time and creation, old as the twelve. Maybe older. He said that it was my dream, if I choose it, but that if I choose it, it ceases to be what it was."

"I don't understand."

"Neither do I, really. I think it means we're making it up now. It's our lives, we're in control. The displacement of time hasn't eliminated our choice. Your choice, Michael. You have to decide what to do."

"I will need time to think."

"We have some, I think."

V: DISTORTION

Michael stood beside the small stream, watching the water run over the stones in clear sheets. He could see himself in a still patch of it. His beard was longer than he liked, his hair messier than a prince should tolerate. The foliage around him had grown dim. He turned from his reflection and looked up through a gap in the trees to see a dark sky, nearing black. On the edge of the expanse he could see a moon rising. There were two in the realm that housed Elosha. One was bright and much like the moon of the World That Is, but the one he watched was a dim red, and very large. In its light, his hands looked warm and flushed.

He heard a shout and the sound of something breaking. He turned his head and listened again. He perceived another shout and realized it was coming from the town. His heart jumped to a quick cadence, his nerves stretching out in sudden tension. He drew his sword and breathed slowly, forcing relaxation upon his ready muscles as he trotted toward the sound. More harsh voices added to the chorus, along with many words Michael did not understand.

When he reached the edge of town he knew that there was an attack underway, though he could not see the fighting. The elf women were scrambling away, past Michael, to where the horses were housed. One of the maidens stopped in front of him, crying out in her strange language. He recognized her as Enatalla's mother. She pointed down the empty space between the stone and wood houses.

Michael nodded and ran, feeling a burst of exhilaration like wind at his back.

He paused as he saw the attackers. They were, at first sight, much like the dark elves, but closer up they looked deformed, almost like a bad drawing of an elf. Their ears hung like dog's, their faces were long and their teeth grotesque, and their were fingers large and misshapen. They wore armor of mail and plate that seemed not to fit any of their hunched bodies, and they carried weapons of rusty steel: swords and spears and wicked axes.

Two male elves were fighting with the attackers, using swords and shields of a simple, old style. Though they fought with great skill, Michael could see behind them many more of the twisted ebenues and knew the elves would soon be overwhelmed. He rushed forward to assist them, but paused again as a blinding wave of magic snaked through them, burning the attackers and confusing them. Michael glanced and saw Shadathal and Afalla, their eyes bright to the point of making his eyes hurt. In their hands they held tools of wood and glass, focuses that with their words caused light to shoot from them, flying into the enemy.

Several of the twisted things appeared from around the trunk of a great tree, right behind Shadathal and Afalla. Michael sprinted toward them, ducking under Shadathal's magical focus. The closest of the creatures was wielding a battle ax, the stroke already winding up to hit Shadathal, who had only just then realized his peril. Michael stepped forward and caught the haft of the swinging ax just below the blade, the force of it jolting his forearm. He gripped the haft tight and pushed the weapon up, the leverage favoring himself. He took another step and planted his right foot past the twisted one, and with a hearty push, it fell backward.

Michael saw the second one, which held a spear, step back from its attack of Afalla and thrust at him. Michael dodged to one side, then took a large step forward with his right foot, extending his sword in a single-handed thrust. The tip caught his attacker in the jugular, even as it swung the spear inward, striking Michael's injured ribs with the haft. It dropped the spear and staggered back, clutching a neck that spurted dark, almost black, blood.

Michael ignored the pain and leapt onto the sprawled attacker he had tripped, half-swording and guiding the wicked tip of his blade into the creature's neck.

"They are running," Shadathal said. Michael turned to see the dark elf, his eyes a blinding white in the dim forest light, casting into the darkness. He turned to look at Michael and his face grew suddenly dimmer and sadder.

Michael felt a hand in his armpit and realized Sharona was helping him to his feet. He stumbled up, wincing at the pain in his ribs.

"You're alright then," he said.

"Yes. More of them were around the side of the house, seeking children, I think. I forestalled them as I could, but my magic does not seem as effective here as it is in the normal world."

"Steel works well enough," Michael said. "Did you see Enatalla?" Michael said.

Sharona shook her head.

Michael grunted in pain. "Her mother couldn't find her."

"They have taken her," Shadathal said softly, in a high, almost whiny, voice.

"Let's get after them," Michael said, dashing toward the woods where two of the dark elves were fighting enemies as they retreated.

"No!" Shadathal called, and Michael turned back. "You cannot!"

Michael stood there in hesitation, but when he saw Sharona running past Shadathal, drawing her arming sword, Michael turned and continued his pursuit, listening for Sharona's footfalls behind him as he tried to keep track of the attackers.

"No! You will get lost!" Michael heard Shadathal call, but he had made his choice.

"That way," Sharona said. Michael looked back and turned where she pointed. He could see shadows slipping through the trees. They went fast, but with their awkward, loping gate, Michael was gaining on them. One of them looked backward, his hazy eyes unreadable. He turned and swung a sword awkwardly at Michael, who parried easily and bowled the creature over.

"There!" Sharona said, and Michael saw the girl being carried by two creatures. He bent his head and sprinted. The creatures paused, as if suddenly pricked. "I'm trying, Michael!"

Michael lunged, and the creature in front stepped back, away from the sword, then swung a club and Michael. Michael slid to one side and chopped at the creature's arm. He flinched as the blade hit and cut clean through the arm; it felt far easier than it should. Blood spilled on the ground and creature let loose a shivering cry. Michael turned his attention just in time to block a sword swing from the other creature.

He stepped back, feeling off balance, but parried two more blows. At last, he had a handle on himself and pressed back, swinging at his enemy's legs, which were bent and unclothed. He struck the creature's shin once, audibly breaking the bone, but that only enraged it, so it began to swing wildly and without control. Michael waited and then stepped in, catching the ragged edge of his opponent's blade on the cross-guard of his sword. As he did so, the creature gave an inhuman wail. Sharona had come in and thrust her own sword into the creature's back.

Michael turned his wrists and felt the quillions on his hilt lock on the creature's sword blade; with a quick twist and pull, he had pulled the sword from its hands. The creature looked at him with vacuous eyes, and Michael took a hardy swing at it, which severed its head cleanly. The body collapsed, pulling Sharona forward with it.

Michael leaned on his sword and caught his breath, feeling the pain in his ribs spring anew. He watched Sharona remove her sword with great effort, then drop it, running to a heap on the ground that was sobbing softly.

"She's alright," Sharona said. "It's Enatalla. She's here."

Michael nodded silently. He looked about himself and saw that a great expanse of trees extended in every direction. "But where is here, eh?" Michael panted.

Sharona leaned back with the elf girl in her arms, trying to catch her own breath. "I don't know, but if Shadathal found us once, I'm sure he can again."

Michael cleaned the dark blood from his blade and sat down beside Sharona, who was talking softly to Enatalla in the broken words of the dark elf language.

"What were those things?" Michael said.

"I can't understand what she's saying about them," Sharona said.

Once Michael had caught his breath, he stood up. "I think we came from this way," he said, pointing off in as near a direction as he thought they had come.

"Yes, I think so," Sharona said. "But the paths may change. Do you remember what Shadathal said?"

"I do," Michael said. "But it's all we can do, isn't it?"

Sharona nodded. "Wait, I can ask Enatalla!" Sharona talked softly to the elf girl, standing her up carefully. She had a cut on her forehead, Michael noticed, and he felt a sudden sadness when looking at it, for he thought it might be deep enough to scar.

"That way," Sharona said, pointing close to the same way Michael had.

They walked with the girl back toward Elosha, or where they supposed it might be. Sharona tore a piece of her dress and kept it pressed against the girl's cut, trying to stop the bleeding. Several times the girl turned them in the forest, until Michael had no idea where they were going. At last, Michael noticed some familiar sights – a bank of the brook, a few hefty needle ash trees, and a wide drift that Michael knew was a path, though it was scattered with leaves.

Michael reached out and grasped Sharona's shoulder.

"What?" Sharona said.

"The leaves are falling off of the trees," Michael said.

Sharona paused and looked around to see a strange autumn of gold and orange leaves, withering and falling from many of the trees around them. Other trees remained full and green – yews and pines – but the maples and beeches, oaks and willows, were all turning to rust.

On they went until they found Elosha among the multihued trees. The leaves there were falling like a soft rain or snow, but one of colors and depth beyond any shower. The lamps outside the many houses were bright in contrast to the trees, which had lost much of their luminosity. The stars and the red moon peeked between the great branches above them as they crossed a little bridge into the town.

Two elves were standing on guard, and both of them nearly dropped their weapons at the sight of the little girl. One ran into the town calling out, and soon Enatalla's mother was rushing out to see them. She gathered the girl up in her arms, luminescent tears falling to the ground. Even as she did this, the rain of leaves seemed to slow.

"What caused this autumn?" Michael said aloud.

"Shadathal," said one of the guards. He gestured for them to follow, and they did, all the way down the lane to the many-faced home of Shadathal, part stone and part living wood.

They found Shadathal in a garden near his house, staring into a small glowing globe that was wrapped in what looked like living wood. He did not take his eyes from the sphere as they stepped through a door to stand near him.

"We've brought back the girl," Michael said.

Shadathal looked up suddenly. "You did? Is she whole?"

"She has a scratch on her face, but otherwise she's fine," Sharona said.

Shadathal nodded and looked at the sphere again.

"What were those things?" Michael said. "They looked like elves, but not."

"The Lost Ones. They've gone dim." He tore his eyes away from the globe and stood up, sighing as he did so. Michael detected lines of worry on his face. "They were like us, once. Part of us. But they lost themselves and their tie to the eternal dream, and have suffered for it. They have never attacked us in our homes so openly. It was a long time coming."

"Why did they try to snatch the girl?" Michael said.

Shadathal looked into Michael's eyes, his own glowing yellow irises searching him. "I cannot say for sure. Or perhaps, I do not want to entertain the reasons."

"Were they actually dark elves?" Sharona said. "They looked… hideous."

"They were. Even as grotesque as they are, I recognize them. I have little power over them, as you saw. Only steel seems to still bite. And your steel bit deep today. You are a great Warrior, Michael. And now I must mourn."

"I didn't realize," Michael said. "I didn't realize they were elves like you."

"They aren't like us anymore," Shadathal said. "Perhaps dispatching them was a mercy; I cannot hold it against you, for it is in your nature to fight against dangers. Yes, it a great mercy, but by my nature, I remember who they were. And I know that it is my fault they died."

He turned his eyes from them and walked inside the house.

*

Michael stood beside Sharona and watched silently as the dead were buried beneath the roots of the bare trees. He watched the faces of the elves, and though many looked sad, they did not cry. No words were spoken, save for the birds that alighted in the trees, of what variety Michael could not discern. When the last shovel-full of earth was thrown on them, the crowd of fair creatures began to disperse and talk to one another again.

"Why did you bury them?" Sharona said to Shadathal as he approached them. "I thought it was your way to inter the dead, so that they might return."

"They had become more like men," Shadathal said. "Those twisted bodies, products of their twisted minds, are not like us. Their spirits are separate, but we still wish to remember them, even as unrecognizable as they are."

"How did they come to be so… deformed," Michael said. He caught a glance from Sharona and added, "Pardon my words."

Shadathal took a breath. "The Prim flows freely in many places here. It is possible, therefore, to reform yourself in it. It is the magic of creation and recreation. You notice that we are not a large tribe, yes?"

Michael nodded.

"We have had many losses over the years. Our children grow up and, disliking the limitation of our home, leave. We are not like the high elves, who came after us. We are not always content with unchanging perfection."

"The high elves are not always content," Sharona said. "They wander Midgard frequently still."

"Perhaps we share that part of our nature with humans," Shadathal said. "That need for danger and novelty. Our children seldom return home, 'tis true. Those beings you fought – the lost ones, are those who left Elosha for other parts of this realm, rather than yours. For a great long time, I did not allow any to leave the realm, because they never returned. We dwindle, you see. So because of my selfishness, our children sought their own powers and their own escape here, in this schism of Niflheim, created by we elders who know the dangers of the mundane world.

"But here there is also a festering darkness, that I did not see until too late. Within the flows of the Prim a few of our dark minds made for themselves a home of twisting corruption. Powerful are those children, who dwell in the outer lands, amid the purest flows of the Prim. The children who followed could not bend that dream to their own will. It bent them, instead. They are our children, you understand, and always they seek to return to us, in whatever form they are cursed to bear."

Michael stood silent. He did not know what to say to Shadathal. At last, he spoke what he had held back since coming. "And what of those who killed my father?"

"They are the dark minds of which I speak. I am sure of it. They hate me for many reasons. For not exerting our power in the world that is, for shutting us away, for what happened to the lost ones."

*

Shadathal approached Michael and Sharona as they ate a soup of vegetables at a table, the nearby window open to let in the eternally muted light, lessened by the loss of foliage.

"You are well?" he said, sitting down.

"I'm back near full strength. Physically, at least." Michael glanced at Sharona.

"I will ask a task of you. You may refuse it," Shadathal said.

"What is it?"

"The assassins must be dealt with."

Michael nodded. "I was wondering if you would ask me to do this."

"It is what you wanted, is it not?"

Michael thought for a moment. "I entertained other thoughts for a time."

"They can help you escape, if you must return. I believe they have something in their possession that allows them to travel to your world, for they themselves lack the magic to depart."

"You cannot free us?" Sharona said.

"I have sealed the way," Shadathal said. "To unseal it risks us."

"What of the lost ones?"

"That is our concern. I cannot save them by forsaking my duty to protect Elosha."

Michael looked at him. "You saw Alanrae - the human woman, correct? She was here and traveled back your realm."

"Yes. You know as I do that it was she who used these… dark minds."

"She could come and return."

"Yes, but I do not know the means. I have sealed the means I know of. Perhaps if she came here, she could free you."

"Unlikely." Michael stared at his soup. "What if I refuse your request?"

"Nothing. You will have to find your own way back."

"Could I stay here?"

Shadathal was quiet for a moment. "You could, but you would no longer be a case for charity."

"I'm not afraid of hard work," Michael said.

"You must consider what is in your nature," Shadathal said. "The two assassins are named Porthil and Mondal. I believe your steel will conquer them, if you choose to use it."

"Why don't you do it yourself?" Michael asked.

"It is against our law and custom to kill another elf. Even the lost ones are a point of great contention. We are not separated, body and soul, as you are." He was silent a moment. "They would not accept punishment willingly."

Sharona said, "What is the punishment usually for murder?"

"Banishment, not death. Of course, one will cause the other, after a time," Shadathal said. "But such is the penalty for murder, which they have committed on behalf of a human."

"So why not banish them?" Sharona said.

"I have tried. They have the same power as I do, as long as they are fed by the flows of the Prim, as all this realm is. They have made their own abode, and I cannot separate them from it with my own knowledge of lightweaving."

"Alanrae must have given them something of great value," Michael said.

"Not necessarily, Michael," Sharona said. "She could have compelled them with magic. Some mages are strong enough to control a person's thoughts and perceptions."

"As my brother reminded me," Michael said. "Though I was a fool to entertain it with you. Let me consider it, Shadathal."

"Of course," the elf said, and rose. He walked calmly out the door.

Michael went back to eating his soup.

"What do you think?" Sharona said.

"My heart says I must see to these men. Elves. My father deserves justice. My heart also aches, for I know that Johan must have been part of this plot. He attacked me because I knew what Alanrae was doing, which means he is part of the conspiracy. He could have betrayed us at the battle, too. He probably did. It makes me sick. Makes my blood burn!" He gripped the spoon in his hand with white knuckles. "I want so badly to not believe any of this, but it is inescapable. I want so badly to avenge my father, and the father of my friend Julia, but I cannot see how I can do it. Once we leave this place, I will be so far beyond the power I need that I cannot fathom what I should do."

Sharona placed her hand gently on Michael. "You are not without power. You have friends, comrades, connections-"

"No title, no money, nobody to call upon for allegiance," Michael interrupted.

"And you have me. I'm pretty good, if I do say so myself."

"And you *do* say so," Michael said. He paused for a moment and watched his soup drip off of his spoon. "And even if I had the power… Johan is my brother. How could I act against him?"

"Act in the way you know best."

"I've never been an outlaw before, I've never-"

"I have," Sharona said. "Oh, don't look so surprised. I don't know what it is, but I have a way of angering people."

Michael smiled slightly. "I'm sure we'll be fine, then." He rapped his knuckles on the table.

"You are still unsure," Sharona said.

"I am."

"You are a warrior, not a farmer."

"Isn't that the sort of question I should answer for myself?"

"Yes, but I'm saving you the trouble, as all good women will."

Michael laughed. "Let's find out where these assassins are. They say revenge is a dish best served cold, but I'm hungry."

"Finish your soup," Sharona said.

Michael chuckled. "It's a metaphor."

"I know. I just think it's bad form to march to possible death whilst hungry." She stood up and stretched her back. "I'll be in the bedroom, when you're finished."

"Why?"

"I think it's bad form to march to possible death whilst hungry," she said again. "Do I have to spell it out for you?"

Michael felt a flush of heat around his neck. "Sharona, I am a nobleman. I would never-"

"You're an outlaw now. So come act like one." She leaned over him and kissed him on the neck, running her hands on his shoulders. "Don't leave me waiting."

With a sigh, she walked out of the little kitchen and down the dark hallway. Michael looked at his soup and hesitated for a few seconds. Then he slurped it all down and got up in a rush, leaving the dirty spoon on the table.

VI: SHARDS OF REALITY

hadathal led them through the mists, the shining bauble of silvery glass in his wand of twisted wood providing light to the path below them, dirty and drifting. The trees above were not aglow, even faintly, like the rest of the realm, but were dark and contained many brown leaves that would not abandon their purchase. The black limbs of these trees writhed around and into each other, like many fingers of uncountable hands. Pinholes of starlight and moonlight drifted through here and there, lighting motes of white dust like tiny rods of white light as they and the horses walked on the bare earth.

The trunks of the trees, too, were of malevolent form. Often, Michael saw, or thought he saw, some face looking back at him from the bark of a tree, but each glimpse was fleeting, and a second glance would dispel the vision, if not the feeling of being watched. Always the faces looked angry or in terrible pain, or sometimes scared. It became cold, and he began to see his breath. He wore clothes that Shadathal had given him, and they felt suddenly inadequate. He glanced over at Sharona, who wore a blue long-sleeved riding dress of similarly thin material. He couldn't help but watch her a moment, taking in the lines of her and watching her breath as she shivered in the dim light.

"How much further?" Sharona said, perched atop Rabble-Rouser. "I shall need a blanket, soon."

"Not far," Shadathal said. "We have entered the forest of malcontent. Porthil and Mondal have dwelt long in resentment of their fellows, in hatred, and here you can see their pain manifest through the Prim. Here the light is truly gone, like the sunless days of yore." His voice began to rise in pitch and tension. "The trees, my memories of the first light – Dead! – and I forget them even as I count them lost. I hate walking here!"

Michael tightened his gloves, partly against the chill and partly in anticipation of the conflict ahead.

"If we keep walking, will we exit the realm?"

"No," Shadathal said. "The cold is the realm of Niflheim encroaching, not the world of men. The mist realm lies beyond the borders, and it is perilous to tread there as a mortal. It is cold and unformed; uncreated. Ah, here we are at last. It has grown more wicked since last I tried to counsel Porthil and Mondal." Shadathal raised a hand and stopped them. They were perched on a hill, looking out into darkness mingled with points of light.

Michael could see below them a sort of house sitting in a patch of pale starlight, but it was unlike any house he had seen before. The front of the house, where stood a large double door, was like the houses of the other elves: beautifully carved and detailed. Beyond that, though, the house looked like it was made of pieces of other more human dwellings. One wall was stone, with irregular windows, bearing a turf roof that turned suddenly to shake as it reached an uneven steeple. Another wall, made of logs and plaster, had a round window and a tile roof, and in many places methods of other construction stood like patches on a quilt. Stone and wood, brick and bone. The house, at its rear, appeared to terminate into the trunk of a massively wide tree, its limbs bereft of any living foliage, but from the cracks in the bark, a soft red light glowed. The stars and a dim moon filtered through, creating a pattern on the bare ground outside like a spider web. Many of the windows bore light of uncanny colors.

"Take this," Shadathal said, and handed a glowing bauble to Sharona. "It will guide you back to the village, if you need to return."

"What if we don't return?" Michael said.

"Then this is our farewell. My life has been enriched by knowing you."

"And mine, whatever happens. Give my thanks to the others."

"I will, but your heroism has earned all hospitality many times over." He bowed and looked into the eyes of each of them, then backed away. Shadathal stepped into the shadows and disappeared among the trees. Soon the footfalls of his horse were lost in the rustling of the wind in the trees.

After a few minutes of watching the house, Michael said, "How shall we approach this?"

"It is up to you," Sharona said. "You are the tactician."

"I would normally say we approach stealthily and try to kill these targets before they become aware of us, but…" he trailed off and narrowed his eyes, watching a shadow in the lighted window. They heard the shouts of an argument.

"But what?" Sharona said quietly.

"But I am not trained in such, nor am I dressed for such. Are you?"

"I can make us silent if we need," Sharona said. "It's not a hard spell. How else do you reckon I slipped away from your brother's soldiers on a warhorse?"

Michael nodded. "Useful." He dismounted and crept closer. Sharona followed him.

"Something else is on your mind," Sharona said.

"It's not the right way to do this. Remember that Shadathal considered banishment. I think he would prefer that, since that is their law."

"You want to give them an ultimatum?"

"It would be the honorable thing to do, but not the smart one."

"Well, are you an honorable man, or a smart man?" She giggled softly.

"What's so funny?"

"That I will get you to answer that question, of course."

Michael took a breath and looked at Sharona's face, lit by the bauble. "I'm an honorable man."

Sharona smiled at him. "Then you know what to do. I will follow your lead."

Michael brought the horses down the muddy hill a few paces and left them tied to a partly rotten tree trunk. They walked out into the yard in front of the house. The image of it seemed to reel slightly; it was bigger than they had thought while standing on the hill, a veritable mansion.

"Porthil and Mondal!" Michael shouted, his hand on his sword. His voice seemed to die in the crackling wind. "Come out and face the judgment of your house."

The wind rose up in greeting, and Michael waited, his hand on his sword, his eyes scanning around him.

They heard a creaking amid the silence, and the trees above seemed to groan and grow. The door opened, and two figures stepped out, each armed with two basket-hilted swords, their blades black as the night that surrounded them. They were armored in tarnished mail and wore masks over their faces, but both had bright yellow eyes like Shadathal.

"Porthil and Mondal," Michael said. "You are to be banished from this realm."

"Did our father put you up to this?" said the elf on the left, who was taller and leaner than the other. He spoke with a high, rasping voice that was almost serpentine. "The old miser."

"They are human, Porthil," said the elf on the right, which Michael presumed to be Mondal. He spoke with a clear, melodious voice, which sounded odd in the dry surroundings. "Perhaps they bring at last the remainder of our payment."

"How could they?" Porthil said. "Our father is the only other besides the woman who can find us."

"I don't know your father," Michael said.

"Oh, I think you do," said Porthil, rolling his shoulders and spinning his swords. "Shadathal is his name."

"I see," Michael said. "He must love you dearly, to not make this threat himself."

"Don't pretend to know the feelings of an elf, especially that one," Porthil said. "His heart is as blackened as any and he will avoid anything that disrupts his comfort."

"He is as he is, brother," said Mondal.

Michael shared a glance with Sharona, then looked back to the elves. "I give you this choice, sons of Shadathal."

"Sons of Pathella!" Porthil said. "I choose to remember her, since my father will not.

"You may leave the realm, or die," Michael continued.

"Some choice," Porthil said.

"Life apart from this nightmare does not seem bad to me," Sharona said.

"You are out of your depth, mortal," Mondal said. "Your choice: turn back, stop being a lapdog for our father, and you may live. Or we will kill you."

"Then I come also to enforce the laws of my own land," Michael said. "Which demand death for assassins! Moreover, I come upon demand of my heart: revenge for my father's blood, which was spilled by you, according to the whim of a wicked woman. A betrayer of the hardest sin."

"He speaks of Alanrae," Mondal said. "Oh, that I could find that woman again." He spun his swords.

"She betrayed us, too," Porthil rasped. "Great promises she made, and none delivered."

"If you sleep with serpents, don't expect to greet the day without a few bites," Sharona said.

Porthil laughed. "Spoken like a slave."

"Regardless of what evil pact you made to slay my father," Michael said. "I am here to deliver justice. You may choose your father's justice, or my justice." Michael drew his sword and fell into a guarded stance. Sharona stumbled back, whispering to herself. She drew her own sword.

"Wait," Mondal said. "I have a proposition."

"I can't imagine one to tempt me," Michael said.

"I'm sure *I* could," Mondal said. "My guess is that you, like us, are prisoners of this realm. Alanrae gave us a magic talisman to travel to the other side, but its magic was exhausted quickly. Quite the ruse on her part. I recognize a mage in your companion."

"If you are trying to bribe me, I could kill you and take the talisman," Michael said.

"Perhaps," Mondal said. "But you risk both your deaths in the process, and we, of course, lose our escape as well, for we lack the magic to excite this artifact – to make it work. I propose a duel, to be fought between you, swordsman, and one of us. If you win, the survivor will provide the talisman and agree to banishment; you have served half your justice and half that of my father. If we win, your companion will leave with both of us, and we keep the talisman. Both of you need not die, and one of you will still escape."

Michael cast a glance at Sharona.

"I would not trust them, Michael."

Michael was silent for a moment, holding his guard. "I agree."

Mondal nodded and looked at Porthil. "Shall we flip for it?"

"I will fight him," Porthil said. "I am the more skilled between us, am I not?"

"You are, but it is only fair we share the risk."

"You think of odds the wrong way, brother. Play your best and assure victory. I will cut this mortal to pieces."

"Do you agree, mortal?" Mondal said.

"My name is Michael. You might as well know it before you die, Porthil." He flourished his sword and set his guard again.

Porthil laughed and strode forward, crossing his swords.

"Be careful Michael!" Sharona said.

"Watch the other one," Michael said.

Porthil came close and fell into a guard, raising one of his twin swords high while keeping the other turned downward. Michael stepped closer.

The two combatants circled one another, eyes locked, the twisting shadows of the tree limbs writhing over their faces. Michael took in his opponent, who was taller and broader than him, his glowing eyes foreign and difficult to read. He still detected in those eyes a mania, which some part of the back of his mind thought would be frightening to most men; to Michael, the mania was an opportunity. He focused on slowing his breathing, keeping his nerves under his control.

Porthil's two swords were masterworks: black with keen, bright single edges, a basket hilt protecting each gloved hand. The elf laughed hoarsely, and rubbed his swords, as if preparing to carve a turkey. Michael's bastard sword was longer than each of those, and he had trained himself to use it single-handedly as well as double; he had the reach advantage and, for whatever lust lived behind Porthil's eyes, the elf guessed this, or he would not be hesitating.

Michael switched from a forward guard to an overhead guard, and Porthil dashed forward, slashing with both swords at once, one swinging high, the other low. Michael leapt back, turning his sword for a quick slash at Porthil's arms. The elf turned his body and stepped backward nimbly, and they circled again.

Michael took a breath, his thoughts racing with possibilities. His mind evaluated every move, from the flick of the sword tips to the assassin's light footwork. One detail stood out.

"This is your last chance," Michael said. "Don't make me kill you."

Porthil laughed and rushed forward.

It played out as Michael had imagined. Porthil flourished his swords in an attempt to confuse him, then attacked with both at once, one high and one low, each with a different arc, in a way that would be impossible to parry or counter normally. Michael lifted his right foot and caught the lower sword with the heel of his boot, the old, stiff leather capturing the keen edge of the black sword like a piece of green wood as the blade bit in. Michael turned his own sword down from his overhead guard and blocked Porthil's upper attack. The swords rang like bells, then sang as steel slid against steel. With a quick turn of his wrist, Michael directed the elf's blow over and away from his body, and with the same motion slammed his bastard sword into Porthil's neck.

Porthil was wearing no gorget, but had a simple mail coif around his head and neck. The links burst as the strong of the sword crushed Porthil's clavicle. The elf cried slightly, shocked, and his right arm seemed to collapse at the sudden loss of strength. His eyes grew to a bright white.

With a quick withdraw, Michael gripped his sword halfway along its length, then swiftly sent the sharp tip of his sword into Porthil's neck, splitting the already broken mail, parting the jack, and severing the elf's carotid artery.

Porthil grunted and swung wildly, frantically, with the sword in his left hand as Michael stepped away. The elf took a step, then fell to his knees, dropping his swords. He swayed for a moment, gazing at nothing, then fell over sideways. His eyes were shocked open, trembling, but he did not move. He stared up at Michael, surprised, and for a few seconds that seemed to stretch until Michael thought time itself would snap, Michael gazed back, feeling a wave of sudden sadness break over his heart, drowning his anger. Then the inner light of Porthil's eyes slowly drained, going from white to pale blue, and he lay still.

"And so it is done," Mondal said coolly. He walked to his brother's body and closed the lifeless eyes, while Michael watched. Michael jumped backward as the earth began to sag beneath Porthil's body. Mondal remained kneeling, unperturbed. The wind picked up, and dead leaves fell from the tree above. The elf's skin began to change texture, and his body became like stems and wood, bark and cone. Within a few seconds, it was part of the ground, then it disappeared.

"Farewell, my brother," Mondal said, and stood up. He pulled down the black cloth mask that covered his face. He looked strikingly like Shadathal, but stronger of feature, harder and in some ways more human. Tears were in his eyes and streaming down his face, glowing.

Mondal took a slow, deep breath and said with a shaky voice, "Come then, mortals. Let us leave this place before it, too, fades."

"What do you mean?" Michael said.

"This place is a creation of Porthil's heart and mind more than mine. Without his spirit here, its details will become lost. So, I fear, shall we. Come, please." Mondal motioned as he walked toward the strange house.

Cautiously, Michael followed. Sharona joined his gate, and he felt her wrap her hands around his arm and squeeze, and heard her breath escaping raggedly.

"This place is not yours, as well?" Sharona said.

"My heart dwells far beyond the realm of Shadathal the Deep," Mondal said. "And beyond it, my heart shall be forever lost, I fear. My brother wanted power over my father. I... I did not care for that. This dream is not mine. I... I am a wasted thing."

They reached the door and walked inside. The interior of the house was as motley as the outside, filled with strange objects and decorations, sick-looking food and drink. Many things hung from the ceiling: feathers, bits of metal, stones, arrowheads, and rings of iron. Mondal picked up an object from a table and handed it to Sharona.

"Here it is," he said. "Alanrae told me it was a focus from the sunless years, but we knew this to be false, for the objects of that time lost their true power forever when light was returned to the world. Still, it permitted us to go and to return, but then it ceased to function."

He handed the object to Sharona. It was a carved stick that had, tied to its end, a ball of glass or crystal, its insides dark.

"Was that the deal you made with her, that you would get this object?" Michael said.

"Part of it," Mondal said. "This was more for Porthil than me, for he wanted to both be free and have his world as he wished it. This would have given him that power. I wonder what this place would have become, had he been able to see more of your world. Would it have become more fair, or less so? The mundane world has its beauty and its sanity, after all."

"What about you?" Sharona said.

Mondal sighed. "I believed a lie, that she could bring back to me one whom I loved, for she has that power. In my heart, I knew it a lie, but I believed it in wickedness. What is love that I could possess it like a trinket?" Mondal stared at his hands. "Already I am changing, without Porthil near me. He was always the stronger one."

The house shook, the wood groaning around them. Mondal picked up a bag and began putting various things into it.

"Let's get back to the horses," Michael said.

"Give me the talisman, so that I know you will not leave me here," Mondal said.

Sharona gripped it tightly. "Just come quickly, Mondal."

Mondal nodded and disappeared into another room. He returned bearing the bag, little more than a leather sack, on his back. In his hand, he clutched a book and a small leather satchel.

"So little?" Michael said.

"I have what I need," Mondal said. "Everything else here is already a burden."

The house began to shake as they walked out the door. The branches swayed and cracked. Leaves blew about them in dark currents, picking up dust. Michael looked back and thought he could hear the cries of fell beasts in the darkness and see the motion of things he had not noticed on his way in, but they were all indistinct and dim.

The trees, black in a gathering mist of white, moved and turned their branches, as if reaching to the moon, as they walked up the hill to where the horses nervously stamped their feet.

"Do you know how to use the talisman?" Mondal said as Michael began untying the horses. "I have little skill in lightweaving, such as it remains in this time as a skill."

"Not quite," Sharona said. "But I think I can guess." She breathed on the ball at the top of the carved wooden handle, and then rubbed it. It sprang to life with an inner fire.

All around them, the dark wood was pushed back into translucence obscured by mist. Through this mist, they could see a familiar moon and stars, and long grass underfoot, slightly blurry.

"Interesting," Sharona said. "It's like the mirror I created, but it projects the world." She ran her hand over the ball again, and the world came into greater clarity. One more breath and the World That Is became reality, the dream of Porthil a vision surrounding them and rippling, like a visual echo. They waited there, listening to the mounting wind. The sight of twisted trees slowly faded, even as the light from the talisman died.

They found themselves standing, with the horses, at the top of a windswept hill. A few gnarled oaks stood on one side, and some miles on the other a woodland began, made of small hardwoods and scrubby brush.

Michael stood and looked around, taking in his bearings. He gasped as Sharona hugged him from the side, pushing her face into his shoulder.

"What is it?" Michael said.

"Just needed to feel you, to know you are real for a moment."

Michael put an arm around her and held her close.

"Where are we?" Sharona said.

"We're far in the west of Ferralla," Michael said. "The plains of Pious's Fall are south of here. Those woods mark the beginning of the Crafter's Mountains that separate the two kingdoms. This is a fortunate place to be."

"How so?" Sharona said.

"Well, we might have come out in the middle of Forgoroto."

"I could have returned my library book," Sharona said, patting her saddlebag.

Michael smiled. He turned and saw Mondal sitting cross-legged on the ground, staring out to the east, where the heart of Ferralla lay.

"What of you, Mondal?" Michael said.

"I don't know," Mondal said. "I thought my sadness would end, stepping out... It has not. Do you know Alanrae?"

Michael chuckled. "I was her betrothed, briefly."

"Then she *does* have the power to possess love."

"It's not like that," Michael said. "What do you know of her?"

"I know she is a powerful sorceress."

"Well, she is also the queen of this country we are standing in, the ruling monarch."

"Then finding her and taking what I am owed will be difficult," Mondal said. "And who are you that you were betrothed to a queen?"

"I am - I was - a prince of a neighboring country, Artalland."

"Named for the great goddess of light?" Mondal said.

Michael clicked his tongue. "Patron goddess of art and aesthetics."

"That which is beautiful to behold."

"Yes."

"Michael, they have different ideas of the gods," Sharona said. "The dark elf gods are older gods, or older versions of the same gods. Oh, and I am Sharona, Mondal. I am… a simple mage."

"Far from simple," Michael said. "Well, Mondal, the countries which surround us now we collectively call the Divine Strand, because once they composed a great empire, the empire of the divine empress, with twelve great provinces. That was a long time ago. Each great city was dedicated to a different of the twelve gods. When the empire fell, that became the means by which each kingdom became named, save for Datalia, which is in truth Naustarium by tradition." He laughed. "This country is Ferralla. To our west, my homeland of Artalland."

"I knew some of this," Mondal said. "But not that Alanrae was a queen. He stood up. His eyes were glowing brightly as he scanned the horizon. "The future is cloudy, and I know not whether I pursue revenge or some other redemption."

"And what about you, Michael?" Sharona said. "Do you seek revenge now?"

"I have seen to the vengeance of my father," Michael said, looking at the assassin as he scanned the hills. "Such as I have a right to."

"You wished now you had killed me too?" Mondal said. "I have no doubt now that you could have."

"No," Michael said softly. "I was right to keep Sharona out of it. If I have any right to revenge, I have none for risking her life, and so I accepted the bargain. There are no debts between us, Mondal. I declare it so."

"Michael, you can always count me in on a fight," Sharona said.

"No," Michael said emphatically. "That is not my way or my wish. Your life does not belong to me."

"But it does…" Sharona said, and turned her head from Michael. "What shall we do?"

"I will go to Artalland first, in secret, and see what aid I may have earned," Michael said. "That is as far as I can plan. If I can procure some charity, you and I could find somewhere else to live."

"You will abandon your rights as prince?" Mondal said. "You are curious, even for a human."

"I have no rights as the second son, and my brother tried to kill me. Altogether, good reasons for finding my own way elsewhere."

"I see. Then we will both be wanderers in this world." Mondal picked up his bag. "Which way shall I go?"

"Anyway you choose," Michael said.

"I have no wisdom for a choice," Mondal said.

"What about the woman you love?" Sharona said. "That is why you entered into a pact with Alanrae, is it not? Why don't you seek her out?"

Mondal looked at her and smiled sardonically. "She is but a dream, from long ago. I don't even know where she is, whether she lives again with another hidden people or has returned to the dream itself."

"Then seek your fortune," Michael said. "There will always be need for warriors."

"Perhaps you are right," Mondal said. "I must trust to destiny, or chance. Good luck to you, Michael. Though there is sorrow in my heart, there is no hatred I have for you. Perhaps one day luck will see us on the same side, rather than as opponents."

With that, Mondal turned and began walking down the hill, to the west.

"There's no such thing as luck," Michael said after him.

Mondal did not answer. Sharona and Michael watched him as he disappeared into the night, losing his shadow amongst the scrubby oak trees.

"I can't believe you let your father's killer go," Sharona said. "Well, I *can* believe it, since I just saw it, but… you know what I mean."

Michael smiled at her. "I pity him, now that I know him. I wonder what long, dark road has made him so wretched."

"And there he walks into the dark," Sharona said.

Michael nodded. "Let us go," he said quietly. "There is a village to the west where we can find vittles, but it will take all the night and most of the day to get there."

"Oh, of course!" Sharona said, thumping her forehead. "We should have gotten food from Shadathal."

"I still have a tack biscuit in my bag," Michael said. "It's not pleasant, but it will keep away the hunger. I am more worried about our clothing, which I think we will find lacking once we're sitting in the cold winds of the mountains." He fingered the thin fabric of his shirt and vest, well-made and beautifully embroidered with an abstract design around the collars and down the sleeves. The green of the shirt held its brilliant color even in the moonlight.

"Don't worry, I packed my old wool dress," Sharona said. "And a few blankets, in case we need to camp. But I think you'll find your clothes adequate. They're a type of silk, spider's silk or so I was told, and are supposed to be good against cold and heat alike. Besides, I like the way they look." She brushed some wrinkles out of her dress, which fell to her ankles in straight lines, covered her arms, and accentuated her hips even as it was loose over her body.

"What about *my* old clothes?"

"I got rid of them," Sharona said. "A good shirt with a large, bloody hole in it is no longer a good shirt."

"My pants?"

"They never fit you well."

Michael laughed.

*

The next day, they reached the small village of Erithice, made of stacked stone turf-roofed houses built along a slow-running river in a valley between two rocky mountains. They were both weary and saddle-sore (for neither of them had done much riding while enjoying the hospitality of Shadathal). Michael had spent much of his time working against his horse, whose name he changed once again from Turner to Trouble in jest. Oddly, the horse seemed to like the name Trouble, responding to it readily.

The people of the village, though they had met Michael long before, did not recognize him. There was still much attention paid to him and Sharona, but for their dress rather than their status, which made the children of the village (who didn't know any better) think they were high elves. The first thing Michael did (after acquiring a hearty supper for himself and Sharona from a homely house), was to set about buying new clothes. He managed, in addition to buying a new jacket of deer hide, to find an old gambeson that a middle-aged man was willing to part with, comforted with knowing that the war was now over.

There they rested for a day and reprovisioned (which came at an inflated cost - the people of Erithice had fallen on hard times since the armies of Ferralla and Artalland had collided nearby the previous autumn, ruining many crops and fields). Their sleep cycles, they found, were not correct; the day-night cycle of turns in the dark elf world had apparently not matched the pattern of the sun. So, it was early on the second morning from their arrival that they woke, sleepless, and decided to set off. The sun was not yet up, and they had not gone to bed late; had either of these things been true they would not have missed the messenger that came in the night bearing important news from the capitol.

Being ignorant, they left the town without disturbing anyone, having paid for all they consumed, and headed up a winding path out of the valley and to a pass in the Crafter's mountains. It wasn't a treacherous path, being well-maintained by the people of Erithice, but it was too narrow for an army to use and made Michael nervous. At the top of the pass, they were able to look forward into the Crafter's mountains, growing smaller and more green as they went west, and were even able to see, far off, fields of crops in Artalland proper.

Night fell soon after clearing the pass, and since Michael and Sharona lacked a tent (for of course neither had bothered to pack one before Johan's attempted assassination), Sharona made a shelter, using her magic, of many boughs of a twisting live oak. This was well, for a thunderhead, moving quickly from the Datalian coast in the south, swept through the mountains and delivered to them both lighting and snow.

The tree limbs above them were soon heavy with the snow, but it filled in the gaps between the leaves and actually improved their function, compared to the time Sharona had tried to put such a thing to use in the rain. They stayed warm (along with both horses, who fit tightly under the shelter) with a small fire Sharona built - a magical one that danced on a pile of stones, which she absent-mindedly changed the colors of every so often.

"What's troubling you?" she said softly as she leaned against Michael.

"Just some things going through my mind," Michael said. "I was wondering how I ended up here, for one; how I could have avoided this outcome."

"I don't begrudge any outcome," Sharona said. She put an arm around his waist. "I have the man I love. I wouldn't have him to hold if things had gone differently."

Michael smiled at her. "I love you, too." He shook his head. "It feels like such an odd thing to say. I've never heard a nobleman talk of loving a woman. Perhaps... perhaps we could travel to *your* home. I don't know much about the Wildlands, but they if they produce people as resourceful as you, I think it would be a decent place to live."

"It *was* decent, but I don't know how it is now."

"Would someone be willing to take us in? Say your parents, while we built something for ourselves?"

"Like I said, I don't know. My parents will be long dead by now."

"Really? How do you know?"

"They would be getting close in age to two hundred by now."

Michael flinched. "What? How?"

Sharona picked her head up and looked at Michael. "I haven't been to the Dobo Wold in well over a hundred years."

"How is that possible? How old are you?"

"I'm… What's the year now?"

"Twenty-five Twenty of the Fourth Dominion."

Sharona thought for a moment. "I'm one hundred and seventy years old," Sharona said. "But don't get fickle just because you're with an older woman. You said you loved me."

"I just…" Michael trailed off. "A hundred and seventy… do all mages live so long?"

"No."

Michael swallowed. "How many… How many men have you had before me?"

"Just one. My husband, Donovo. He died before I left the Wold."

"I'm sorry," Michael said.

"Don't be. He was a good man, and our time was brief and well-lived, but all things happen for a reason. And I now I have you." She leaned up and kissed his face. "I love you much more, if you wish to know."

"Doesn't that… feel a bit… odd? Like you're insulting his memory to say and feel that?"

"He's not here to be insulted, Michael. He was the fleeting glimpse of a life I wasn't meant to have. His death sent me on my journey. You must have had other women, surely, being a prince."

"If you were anyone else I would lie and say not," Michael said. "But truthfully it has been only one other, and I regret it."

"Why?"

"I took what should have been reserved for her husband. I dishonored myself by letting her… By letting her believe that she could have a prince. For more than a few nights, I mean. It was a vicious thing to do."

"I see," Sharona said. "Well, I forgive you for knowing another woman."

"It is *she* who should forgive me, not you."

"I am forgiving what *you* gave away, that you should have reserved for *me*."

Michael laughed softly. "You are a strange woman. If you are truly one-hundred seventy-"

"I am not lying Michael. Have I ever?"

"No." He cleared his throat. "How did you live to be so... old?"

"I shall forgive you for calling a lady old," Sharona said. " but truthfully, most of the time I was... lost in a pocket of the Fay Lands. I was dreaming, and wandering in real dreams. It gave me long life, to dream and then fulfill the dream, I thought. Always my dreams were about a man. A man that I was supposed to follow. He needed me, at the least to protect him, for I saw him in chains or worse when I did not see myself beside him. A man that, through all the visions I saw of him and of me, which are now fading from my mind, I came to love beyond all hope and reason, for though I witnessed his virtue and his strength, I also saw in the dream that he was a great prince, even a king. And how could a *king* love *me*?"

"A king could love you because of who you are – your honesty and your loyalty. A king could love you because of your devotion, because you save him, over and over. But I am not a king, Sharona. I am not even a prince, anymore."

"You are a greater man than the king," Sharona said. "And you are yet young. Perhaps you will be a king. I saw it. Or, I think I did. Since I walked away all those years ago the dream has haunted me, torturing me with visions of a man I loved but would probably never know, and now it fades." Suddenly, Michael felt her weeping, her chest heaving as she leaned against him. She pounded her fist on his chest softly. "I love you more than in the dream. So much more. It is like comparing a reflection of the sky in a pond to the real thing. Who you are is so much better than the dream, but I just need to see it again, so I can know what to do."

"I suppose it is up to me to decide what we shall do," Michael said. "You will have me, whatever I decide. I promise."

"Good." Sharona took a breath and wiped the tears from her face with her sleeve. "I am sorry. I have talked about myself, and not what is troubling you."

"Don't worry about me."

"That's all I do, Michael, and I'm fairly certain you don't mean that, or you'd likely be dead at the hands of your brother."

"True. Very well, I am thinking that I am very bad at politics, and had I followed my brother's lead, things would be alright. He tried very hard to give me the right advice, once, and part of me wishes I had taken it."

"What about the other part?"

"I'm glad I didn't, for I know my brother more truly now. And that is not a worthless thing, for who can say he truly knows another man? I know why he tried to kill me, and it was because I knew Alanrae was responsible for my father's death. He killed my father, as much as if his own hand had committed the deed, by colluding with the queen. I could not have avoided this, but is there a lesson I can learn so I can bring justice to my father?"

"You can only be who you are, Michael. I would not have you be like your brother."

"I would never murder my father for the sake of ambition," Michael said, "so I will never be like him. But that doesn't mean some parts of what he did and what he knows are without merit. Just as an enemy can have valid sword techniques, so too can he have valid understandings and approaches in the political world. There is something else, though."

"What?"

"I look at my brother, and all he did, and I wonder if I could be as proficient a king as he. If I could manage the intrigue. He may be the better king. Do I owe it to my kingdom to give it the best king?"

"Does an evil man have the capacity to rule with moral righteousness? To uphold the law he is charged to oversee?" Sharona said. "That's not rhetorical. I truly do not know. You're the first prince I've ever met."

Michael laughed. "I don't know either, but I don't think it is as cut and dry as that. To do right, you must have the power to do right; to have that power, you must… act along a different set of dictums for behavior. Perhaps." He was silent for a few minutes, rubbing gently Sharona's shoulders. Then he said, "I think I will go to Angelico's estate, here in the eastern Hinterlands. If any family would lend me aid, it is the Travisti family."

"Then where?"

Michael smiled. "The Travistis are as clever and old a clan as exists. They will know how to bring justice to my brother, if it is even possible."

"The path is set, then," Sharona said. "The warrior prince returns home."

Michael smiled. "Yes, home. Now I believe it is time for something that should have no debate on my part." He leaned over and kissed her, then she fell backward with him to the bedroll.

END OF BOOK II

ABOUT THE AUTHOR

David Van Dyke Stewart is an author, musician, YouTuber, and educator who currently lives in Modesto, California with his wife and son. He received his musical education as a student of legendary flamenco guitarist Juan Serrano and spent the majority of his 20s as a performer and teacher in California and Nevada before turning his attention to writ-

ing fiction, an even older passion than music. He is the author of *Muramasa: Blood Drinker*, a historical fiction novel set in feudal japan, *Water of Awakening*, a fantasy novel told in the classic style, and *Prophet of the Godseed*, a hard-scifi novel that focuses on the consequences of relativity in space travel, as well as numerous novellas, essays, and short stories.

You can find his YouTube channel at http://www.youtube.com/rpmfidel where he creates content on music education (including extensive guitar lessons), literary analysis, movie analysis, philosophy, and logic.

Be sure to check http://davidvstewart.com and http://dvspress.com for news and free samples of all his books. You can join his mailing list for advanced access to upcoming content at http://dvspress.com/list

Printed in Great Britain
by Amazon

30373176R00063